John Lyly's Love's Metamorphosis: A Retelling

David Bruce

Published by David Bruce, 2022.

JOHN LYLY'S LOVE'S METAMORPHOSIS: A RETELLING

First edition. September 29, 2022.

Copyright © 2022 David Bruce.

ISBN: 979-8215618271

Written by David Bruce.

Table of Contents

Dedication

Dedicated to Carl Eugene Bruce and Josephine Saturday Bruce

My father, Carl Eugene Bruce, died on 24 October 2013. He used to work for Ohio Power, and at one time, his job was to shut off the electricity of people who had not paid their bills. He sometimes would find a home with an impoverished mother and some children. Instead of shutting off their electricity, he would tell the mother that she needed to pay her bill or soon her electricity would be shut off. He would write on a form that no one was home when he stopped by because if no one was home he did not have to shut off their electricity.

The best good deed that anyone ever did for my father occurred after a storm that knocked down many power lines. He and other linemen worked long hours and got wet and cold. Their feet were freezing because water got into their boots and soaked their socks. Fortunately, a kind woman gave my father and the other linemen dry socks to wear.

My mother, Josephine Saturday Bruce, died on 14 June 2003. She used to work at a store that sold clothing. One day, an impoverished mother with a baby clothed in rags walked into the store and started shoplifting in an interesting way: The mother took the rags off her baby and dressed the infant in new clothing. My mother knew that this mother could not afford to buy the clothing, but she helped the mother dress her baby and then she watched as the mother walked out of the store without paying.

My mother and my father both died at 7:40 p.m.

Cover Photograph for John Lyly's *Love's Metamorphosis*: A Retelling: Adina Voicu

https://pixabay.com/photos/girls-friend-three-dresses-beauty-1487826/

***

Educate Yourself
    Read Like A Wolf Eats
    Be Excellent to Each Other
    Books Then, Books Now, Books Forever

***

In this retelling, as in all my retellings, I have tried to make the work of literature accessible to modern readers who may lack some of the knowledge about mythology, religion, and history that the literary work's contemporary audience had.

Do you know a language other than English? If you do, I give you permission to translate this book, copyright your translation, publish or self-publish it, and keep all the royalties for yourself. (Do give me credit, of course, for the original retelling.)

I would like to see my retellings of classic literature used in schools, so I give permission to the country of Finland (and all other countries) to buy (or get free) one copy of this eBook and give copies to all students forever. I also give permission to the state of Texas (and all other states) to buy (or get free) one copy of this eBook and give copies to all students forever. I also give permission to all teachers to buy (or get free) one copy of this eBook and give copies to all students forever.

Teachers need not actually teach my retellings. Teachers are welcome to give students copies of my eBooks as background material. For example, if they are teaching Homer's *Iliad* and *Odyssey*, teachers are welcome to give students copies of my *Virgil's* Aeneid: *A Retelling in Prose* and tell students, "Here's another ancient epic you may want to read in your spare time."

CAST OF CHARACTERS

MAIN GODS

Cupid, God of Love.

Ceres, Goddess of Agriculture.

FORESTERS

Ramis, in love with Nisa. The Latin word *ramus* means "branch."

Montanus, in love with Celia. The Latin word *montanus* means "mountaineer."

Silvestris, in love with Niobe. The Latin word *silva* means "forest."

OTHER MORTAL CHARACTERS

Erisichthon, a churlish farmer.

Protea, daughter to Erisichthon.

Petulius, in love with Protea.

NYMPHS OF CERES

Nisa. Nisa believes that she can resist any man. She does not believe that true love exists. Ramis thinks that she mocks love.

Celia. Celia wants to stay beautiful and not have children. Montanus thinks that she hates love.

Niobe. Niobe does not want to have just one man. She hates — or says she hates — the kind of love that leads to loyalty and chasteness. Silvestris thinks that she thinks she is above love.

Tirtena. Tirtena speaks only one line in the play.

Fidelia, transformed into a tree.

MINOR CHARACTERS

A Merchant.

A Siren.

The Scene: Arcadia. A rustic area.

The play makes a few references to Thessaly.

Thessaly is in northern Greece, and Arcadia is in southern Greece in the central Peloponnesus.

Arcadia is also a fictionalized rustic area.

The Arcadia in the play has a seashore, but the Arcadia in southern Greece in the central Peloponnesus does not have a seashore.

Thessaly does have a seashore.

Erisichthon was a king of Thessaly, but in this play Erisichthon is a rich farmer.

NOTES:

Peter Lukacs has excellently edited and annotated this play. It can be downloaded free here:

http://elizabethandrama.org/the-playwrights/john-lyly/loves-metamophosis-by-john-lyly/

Leah Scragg has also excellently edited and annotated this play:

Lyly, John. *Love's Metamorphosis.* Ed. Leah Scragg. Manchester, UK: Manchester University Press. Distributed exclusively in the USA by Palgrave Macmillan, 2008.

ROMAN NAME (GREEK NAME)

Bacchus (Dionysus): god of wine and ecstasy

Ceres (Demeter): goddess of grain and agriculture

Cupid (Eros): god of love; also, son of Venus

Diana (Artemis): goddess of the hunt

Juno (Hera): wife of Jupiter, king of the gods, and so she is queen of the gods

Jupiter, aka Jove (Zeus): king of the gods

Mercury (Hermes): a messenger-god

Neptune (Poseidon): god of the sea

Proserpine (Persephone): wife of Pluto, god of the Land of the Dead; also, daughter of Ceres

Pluto (Hades): god of the Land of the Dead

Ulysses (Odysseus): hero of Homer's epic poem *Odyssey*

Venus (Aphrodite): goddess of sexual desire

Vesta (Hestia): goddess of the hearth

CHAPTER 1

— 1.1 —

Three foresters — Ramis, Montanus, and Silvestris — talked together while standing by a tree that was sacred to Ceres, the goddess of agriculture. The foresters, whose job was to take care of the woods on this estate, were carrying shields and garlands. Garlands are wreathes made of flowers and leaves. These garlands would be hung on Ceres' sacred tree to honor Ceres. The shields were heraldic shields and bore designs that told which nymph each forester loved.

Another name for shields is escutcheons.

The three foresters had fallen in love with three nymphs. Nymphs are long-lived minor deities of nature.

Ramis loved Nisa, Montanus loved Celia, and Silvestris loved Niobe. Unfortunately, the three nymphs did not return their love.

Ramis said, "I cannot see, Montanus, why it is fabled by the poets that Love sat upon the chaos and created the world, since in the world there is so little love."

Different mythologies have different creators who bring order out of chaos. In this mythology, Love performs that creation. This Love is not Cupid, god of Love. This philosophical and perhaps religious Love is much stronger. Cupid was created and is part of the universe.

"Ramis, thou cannot see that which cannot with reason be imagined," Montanus said, "for if the divine virtues of Love had dispersed themselves through the powers of the world so forcibly as to make them take by his influence the forms and qualities impressed within them, no doubt they could not choose but savor more of his divinity."

In other words: Using reason, we can conclude that if Love created the world, then love ought to permeate all of existence.

Silvestris said:

"I do not think Love has any spark of divinity in him, since the end of his being is earthly: In the blood he is born by the frail fires of the eye, and he is quenched by the frailer shadows of thought."

According to Silvestris, Love need not be regarded as a god. We look at someone and are attracted to them, and Love is born. But then our reason may let us know that this person is not a suitable partner for us, and Love dies.

Silvestris continued:

"What reason have we then to pander to his desires with such zeal, and follow his fading delights with such passion?"

Another conception of love is Cupid, the god of love who shoots gold arrows at people and makes them fall in love.

Because Silvestris, like Ramis and Montanus, has been rejected by the nymph he loves, he thinks that Love, aka Cupid, offers fading delights. First we have the delights of falling in love, followed by the pain of rejection.

Ramis said, "We have bodies, Silvestris, and human bodies, which in their own natures being much more wretched than beasts, do much more miserably than beasts pursue their own ruins; and since it will ask longer labor and study to subdue the powers of our blood — our passion and lust — to the rule of the soul, than to satisfy them with the fruition of our loves, let us be constant in the world's errors, and seek our own torments."

In other words: As humans, it is in our character to fall in love. Subjecting our passions and lust to the rule of reason would require much effort and study, and so it is better to continue to fall in love and try to have our love reciprocated even though the attempt will often fail and leave us in torment.

Montanus said:

"It is as good to yield indeed submissively, and satisfy part of our affections, as to be stubborn without the ability to resist, and to enjoy none of them."

By pursuing the person we love, we will at least be doing what our heart wants us to do. That is some satisfaction even if we are rejected.

Montanus continued:

"I am in the worst plight, since I love a nymph who mocks love."

"And I love a nymph who hates love," Ramis said.

"I love a nymph who thinks herself above love," Silvestris said.

Ramis said:

"Let's not argue about whose mistress — whose loved one — is the baddest, since they are all cruel; nor let us argue about which of our fortunes are the most perverse, since they are all desperate and hopeless."

In this sense, "mistress" means "woman who is loved."

Ramis continued:

"I will hang my shield on this tree in honor of Ceres, and I will write this verse on the tree in hope of my success:

"*Penelopen ipsam perstes, modo tempore vinces.*

"Penelope will yield at last: continue and conquer."

The Latin quotation is from Ovid, *Ars Amatoria* (*The Art of Love*), Book 1, line 477.

Translated, the quotation says, "If you are persistent, you will conquer Penelope herself in time."

Ulysses' wife, Penelope, remained chaste during the twenty years that her husband spent away from home. The first ten years he spent fighting the Trojan War, and the second ten years he spent trying to get back home. Much of that time he was kept captive on an island by the goddess Calypso.

During much of that time, people assumed that Ulysses was dead, and over 100 suitors tried to convince Penelope to marry one of them. Penelope was able to hold them off for some time with her famous weaving trick. She told them that after she had woven a shroud for Ulysses' father, Laertes, she would choose one of them to marry. Each day she wove the shroud, and each night she unwove what she had woven.

All of the foresters would hang their shields on the tree to honor Ceres, and they would write short mottos or verses on the garlands and hang them on the tree to honor Ceres.

Montanus said:

"I will write this verse on the tree:

"*Fructus abest facies cum bona teste caret.*

"Fair faces lose their beauty, if they accept no lovers."

The Latin quotation is from Ovid, *Ars Amatoria* (*The Art of Love*), Book 3, line 398.

Translated, the quotation says, "The fruit is absent from the face when it lacks a good witness."

Ramis asked Silvestris, "But why are thou thinking so hard? What will thou write for thy lady to read?"

Silvestris answered:

"That which necessity forces me to endure: to revere love, and to admire wisdom:

"*Rivalem patienter habe.*"

The Latin quotation is from Ovid, *Ars Amatoria* (*The Art of Love*), Book 2, the first half of line 539.

Translated, the quotation says, "Be patient with your rival."

Montanus then suggested that they go to work in their separate parts of the forest: "Come, let us all go to our walks. Perhaps we shall meet the nymphs walking."

The three nymphs — Nisa, Celia, and Niobe — walked over to the tree that was sacred to Ceres.

"It is time to hang up our garlands," Nisa said. "This is our harvest holyday: On this festival day, we must both sing and dance in honor of Ceres. Of what colors or flowers is thine garland made of, Niobe?"

Niobe said:

"Of salamints, which are white in the morning, red at noon, and purple in the evening, for in my affections there shall be no staidness but in unstaidness."

Staidness is constancy. The salamint — a flower that John Lyly made up — is not constant in color. Niobe wanted to be constant only in inconstancy. That is, she didn't want to be tied to only one relationship, but to go from one relationship to another, or to have many relationships at the same time.

Niobe then asked:

"But what is yours of, Nisa?"

Nisa said:

"My garland is made of holly because it is most holy and its lovely green neither the sun's beams, nor the wind's blasts, can alter or diminish."

Holly is not affected by the elements, and Nisa is not affected by men. For Nisa, romantic love does not exist.

Nisa then asked:

"But, Celia, what garland do you have?"

Celia answered, "Mine is made all of cypress leaves, which are broadest and most beautiful, yet bear the least fruit; for beauty makes the brightest show, being the slightest substance; and I am content to wither before I am worn and to deprive myself of that which so many desire: sex."

The cypress is very beautiful but bears little fruit, and Celia was content to be beautiful but have no children. She knew that her beauty would wither eventually, but she was content to have her beauty wither before she had children. She was content to die a virgin.

Niobe said:

"Come, let us make an end to this discussion, lest Ceres comes and finds us slack in performing that which we owe her: music and dancing."

Noticing the writing on Ceres' sacred tree, Niobe said:

"But wait, some people have been here this morning before us."

"The amorous foresters, or no one, have been here," Nisa said, "for in the woods they have eaten so much wake-robin, that they cannot sleep for love."

Wake-robin is an herb that people used when they suffered from depression.

"Alas, poor souls, how ill love sounds in their lips, who by telling a long tale of hunting, think they have revealed a sad passion of love!" Celia said.

The foresters didn't know how to tell a nymph that they loved her, and so they talked about hunting instead and hoped that each nymph understood that she was loved.

Oddly enough, this worked, because the three nymphs knew that the three foresters loved them.

Niobe said, "Give them permission to love, since we have liberty to choose whom we will love or not love, for I take as great entertainment in coursing their tame hearts, as they take pains in hunting their wild harts."

The verb "to course" can mean 1) to hunt, 2) to chase, or 3) to trouble.

Niobe delighted in teasing the forester who loved her.

Celia said:

"Niobe, your affection is only pinned to your tongue, which when you wish you can unloose."

Niobe's love is not real love, but just teasing: She can easily "love" someone other than the forester who loves her.

Celia then said:

"But let us read what they have written: *Penelopen ipsam perstes modo tempore vinces.*

"That is for you, Nisa, whom nothing will move, yet hope makes him hover."

Ramis, who loved Nisa, had placed the motto "If you are persistent, you will conquer Penelope herself in time" on Ceres' tree.

Nisa was the nymph who thought she could resist any man.

"A fond hobby to hover over an eagle," Nisa said.

A hobby is a type of falcon; eagles were regarded as a better bird.

Nisa regarded herself as the eagle, and she regarded Ramis as the hobby.

The word "fond" can mean "foolish."

Niobe said:

"But foresters think all birds are buntings."

Buntings are small colorful birds. "Foresters think all birds are buntings" metaphorically meant that they think that all women are alike.

Niobe then said:

"What's the next motto? *Fructus abest facies cum bona teste caret.* Celia, the forester gives you good counsel: Take your pennyworth while the market serves."

In other words: Sell while there is a demand.

Or: Find a husband while you are young and beautiful.

Montanus, who loved Celia, had hung the motto "The fruit is absent from the face when it lacks a good witness" on Ceres' tree.

Celia was the beautiful nymph who wished never to have children.

"I hope it will be market day until my death's day," Celia said.

She hoped to remain beautiful until she died.

The verb "hope" can mean "expect."

Nisa said:

"Let me read, too: *Rivalem patienter habe.*

"He touches you, Niobe, to the quick, yet you see how patient he is in your inconstancy."

Silvestris, who loved Niobe, had hung the motto "Be patient with your rival" on Ceres' tree.

Niobe said:

"Inconstancy is a vice that I will not swap for all the virtues; although I throw a man off with my whole hand, I can pull him back again with my little finger."

Niobe wanted to have many lovers. Getting rid of a lover might require effort, but getting a new lover was easy.

Niobe then said:

"Let us encourage them, and write something: If they judge it favorably, we will know that they are fools; if they respond with anger, we will say they are perverse."

Niobe wanted the nymphs to tease the foresters by leaving messages for them.

Nisa said:

"I will begin.

"*Cedit amor rebus, res age, tutus eris.*"

The Latin quotation is from Ovid's *Remedia Amoris* (*The Cures for Love*), line 144.

Translated, the quotation says, "Love gives way to things, keep busy, you will be safe."

In other words: Keep busy, and you can avoid falling in love.

Celia said:

"Indeed, it is better to count the stars than to be idle, yet it is better to be idle than to be ill-employed.

"My motto is this: *Sat mihi si facies, sit bene nota mihi.*"

The Latin is a variation of a line from Ovid's *Heroides* (*Heroines*) xvii.38.

Translated, the Latin means, "If you will pursue me, let it be well known to me."

One way for Montanus to do that would be to praise Celia's beauty.

Niobe said, "You care for nothing but a glass — that is, a flatterer."

A glass is a mirror, and flatterers praise a woman's beauty.

"Then all men are glasses," Nisa said.

"Some glasses are true," Celia said.

Sometimes, when a man praises a woman's beauty, her beauty really is worthy of praise.

Niobe said:

"No men are true glasses: All men are liars."

She then said:

"But this is my motto: *Victoria tecum stabit.*"

The Latin quotation is from Ovid, *Ars Amatoria* (*The Art of Love*), Book 2, the second half of line 539 and the first word of line 540.

Translated, the quotation says, "Victory rests with you."

Silvestris' motto had been the first half of line 539:

"*Rivalem patienter habe.*"

Nisa said, "Thou give hope to Silvestris."

"He who is patient is worthy of it," Niobe said.

Silvestris' motto, translated, had been: "Be patient with your rival."

Celia said:

"Let us sing, and so attend on Ceres; for this day, although into her heart never entered any impulse of love, yet usually to the temple of Cupid, she offers two white doves, as asking for his favor, and one eagle as commanding his power."

Ceres was actually a mother: Her daughter was Proserpine, aka Persephone. Perhaps, however, Ceres had not yet become a mother at this time.

Doves are associated with Cupid's mother, Venus, and eagles are associated with Jupiter, the king of the gods.

Turtledoves mate for life.

"To command his power" can mean to ask for his protection.

Since Ceres is a goddess, such a request is likely to be at least strongly considered.

Celia then said:

"*Praecibusque minas regaliter addet.*"

Translated, the Latin means, "She will add threats to her royal entreaties."

When dealing with Cupid, Ceres used both the carrot and the stick.

The nymphs sang and danced to honor Ceres.

Erisichthon, a wealthy and churlish farmer whose estate contained these woods, entered the scene and said:

"What noise is this, what assembly, what idolatry?

"Has the modesty of virgins turned to wantonness?

"Is the honor of Ceres now considered to be immoral?

"And is Erisichthon, the ruler of this forest, now believed to have no power?

"You are impudent giglots — harlots — to disturb my game animals or to dare do honor to any but Erisichthon. It is not your fair faces as smooth as jet — black marble — nor your enticing eyes, even if they drew and attracted iron like adamantine magnets, nor your polished speeches, even if they were as forcible as Thessalides', that shall make me any way flexible."

"Thessalides'" may be a typo for "Thessalians," meaning the women of Thessaly.

Aglaonice or Aganice of Thessaly is regarded as the first female astronomer of ancient Greece. She and some women associated with her became known as "the witches of Thessaly."

She claimed to be able to "make the Moon disappear from the sky," which is now interpreted as meaning that she could predict lunar eclipses. Her words and the words of the women in her scientific group would be well worth hearing.

Niobe said:

"Erisichthon, thy stern looks combined with thy haughty speeches, thy words as unkempt as thy locks of hair, were able to frighten men of bold courage, and to make frantic us simple girls, who are full of fear; but know thou, Erisichthon, that if thy hands were as ungoverned and unrestrained as is thy tongue, and the one was as ready to execute and perform evil as the other — your tongue — was to threaten it, it should neither move our hearts to ask for pity, or remove our bodies from this place.

"We are the handmaids of divine Ceres. To fair Ceres is this holy tree dedicated — to Ceres, by whose favor thyself live, who deserve to perish."

Erisichthon was a farmer, and Ceres was the goddess of agriculture. Erisichthon owed his livelihood to Ceres.

Erisichthon said:

"Are you so devoted to Ceres that to spite Erisichthon, you will engage in these sacrificial offerings?"

The sacrificial offerings included the nymphs' song and their dance, but Erisichthon may have been referring to the mottos on Ceres' holy tree.

The ancient Greeks did sacrifice animals to honor the gods, but the sacrifices in this play are offerings that do not involve the killing of animals.

Erisichthon continued:

"No, immodest girls, you shall see that I have neither the regard for your sex that men should tender to you, nor of your beauty that foolish love would dote on, nor of your goddess, which no one except peevish, foolish girls reverence and honor."

Erisichthon did not love: This was an affront to Cupid.

Erisichthon continued:

"I will destroy this tree to spite all; and so that you may see my hand execute what my heart intends, and so that you realize that nothing may appease my malice, my last word shall be the beginning of the first blow."

Erisichthon struck the tree with his axe.

"Oh, alas! What has he done!" Celia said.

"We ourselves, I fear, must also provide matter to feed his fury!" Niobe said.

The nymphs could attempt to physically stop Erisichthon from cutting down Ceres' sacred tree.

"Let him alone," Nisa said, "but look, the tree pours out blood, and I hear a voice."

In Virgil's *Aeneid*, Aeneas was looking for a home for himself and the other Trojan survivors of the Trojan War. He landed in Thrace and thought to build a city there, but in a thicket of dogwood and myrtle he broke a branch off a tree and blood poured out. He heard a voice and learned that the voice was that of Polydorus, a prince of Troy, who said to him:

"Why, Aeneas, are you making me bleed? Spare me, and spare yourself. No good can come to you from fouling your hands with my blood. You know me. I am a Trojan, and the blood you see is Trojan. Escape from this guilty land. I am Polydorus, and I am one of the sons of Priam. Here I was murdered with spears. The spears stayed in my body after my death. They took root and grew."

This was a bad omen, and the Trojans left Thrace, but first they built a proper burial mound for Polydorus.

Dante, of course, knew Virgil's *Aeneid* well, and he used the image of a tree speaking when a branch is broken in his *Inferno* in the section about the suicides. (Of course, Polydorus was a murder victim, not a suicide.)

After leaving a river of boiling blood where the violent against other people were punished, Dante and Virgil arrived at a gloomy wood where the Suicides were punished. The Suicides were the grubby shrubs of the wood. They could communicate only when a twig or branch was broken, and then they used the resulting hole as a mouth until the blood congealed.

This punishment was appropriate because by killing themselves, the Suicides had given up the privilege of self-determination. As shrubs, the Suicides had no free will because plants have no free will. This was appropriate because in life the Suicides had rejected free will by committing suicide. As grubby shrubs, the Suicides could not move around and could not even speak unless someone broke off a twig or branch. At the Last Judgment, the Suicides will be given back their bodies, but because they had rejected their bodies when they were alive, the bodies will hang from the branches of the shrubs.

Erisichthon asked:

"What voice?"

He then said to the tree:

"If in the tree there is anybody, speak quickly, lest the next blow hit the tale out of thy mouth."

The voice of the transformed nymph Fidelia came from the trunk of the tree:

"Monster of men, hate of the heavens, and to the earth a burden, what transgression has chaste Fidelia committed?

"Is it thy spite, Cupid, who, having no power to wound my unspotted, pure, chaste mind, procured means and found a way to mangle my tender body, and by violence to gash those sides that enclose a heart dedicated to virtue?"

Fidelia was asking whether Cupid, god of Love, had inspired Erisichthon to cut that tree that was actually Fidelia. Cupid's motive for doing that would be Fidelia's desire to remain a virgin and not lie with a man.

Fidelia continued:

"Or is it that savage satyr, who feeding his sensual appetite upon lust, seeks now to quench it with blood, so that since he is without hope to attain my love, he may with cruelty end my life?"

Satyrs were half-man and half-goat, and they were notoriously lustful. A satyr had pursued Fidelia but had not succeeded in bedding her.

Fidelia continued:

"Or does Ceres, whose nymph I have been for many years, in recompence and repayment of my inviolable faith, 'reward' me with unspeakable torments?

"Divine Phoebus Apollo, who pursued Daphne until she was turned into a bay tree, ceased then to trouble her. Aye, the gods are full of pity."

The ancient Greek gods, including Zeus and Apollo, were notoriously lustful, and they slept with many mortal women and immortal goddesses. They were entirely capable of rape.

Zeus' Roman name is Jupiter.

Apollo had pursued Daphne, who prayed for an escape from him. Her father, the river god Peneus of Thessaly, heard her prayer and turned her into a bay laurel tree.

Fidelia continued:

"Cinyras, who with fury followed his daughter Myrrha until she was changed to a myrrh tree, ceased then to torment her. Yes, parents are natural."

Parents naturally love their children. Here, the love is shown by her father's ceasing to torment her once she was transformed.

Myrrha had an unnatural love for her father, Cinyras, and when he was drunk, she committed incest with him. Their child was the beautiful Adonis. Her father chased after her with a sword. Myrrha asked the gods to transform her into something other than a human being, and they transformed her into a myrrh tree.

Fidelia continued:

"Phoebus Apollo lamented the loss of his friend, Cinyras, who lost his child.

"But both gods and men either forget or neglect the transformation of Fidelia; indeed, they follow her after her transformation so they can make her more miserable.

"The result is that there is nothing more hateful than to be chaste. The bodies of the chaste women are followed in the world with lust, and then they are tormented in the graves with tyranny.

"The freer the minds of the chaste are from vice, the more their bodies are in danger of evil being done to them, so that they are not safe when they live, because of men's love.

"Nor are they safe after being changed and transformed, as I was into a tree, because of their hates.

"Nor are they safe when they are dead because their reputations are defamed and slandered.

"What is that chastity which so few women study ways to keep, and both gods and men seek to violate?

"If chastity is only a naked name — just a word — why are we so superstitious about and so devoted to a hollow sound?

"If chastity is a splendid virtue, why are men so negligent in respecting such an exceeding splendidness?

"Go, ladies, tell Ceres that I am that Fidelia who for so long made garlands in her honor, and chased by a satyr, by prayer to the gods became turned into a tree; whose body now is grown over with a rough bark, and whose golden locks are covered with green leaves; yet whose mind nothing can alter, neither the fear of death, nor the torments of death."

Her mind did not change: Her mind was still human.

Fidelia continued:

"If Ceres will seek no revenge, then let virginity be not only the scorn of savage people, but the spoil. Let savage people despise virginity and take virgins' virginity.

"But, alas, I feel the last of my blood come. I am soon to die, and therefore I must end my last breath.

"Farewell, ladies, whose lives are subject to many evils; for if you are beautiful, it is hard to be chaste.

"If you are chaste, it is impossible to be safe and remain a virgin.

"If you are young, you will quickly bend.

"If you bend, you are suddenly broken.

"If you are ugly, you shall seldom be flattered and complimented.

"If you are not flattered, you will always be sorrowful.

"Beauty is a firm fickleness, youth is a feeble staidness, deformity is a continual sadness."

In other words: Beauty is always variable; it always leaves us. Young people are weak when it comes to virtue. Deformity always causes sadness.

Being turned into a tree can be regarded as a kind of deformity.

Fidelia died.

Niobe said to Erisichthon, "Thou monster, can thou hear this without grief?"

Erisichthon said, "Yea, and I can double your griefs with my blows."

He cut the tree until it fell to the ground.

Nisa said, "Ah, poor Fidelia, the perfect model of chastity and example of misfortune!"

Celia said, "Ah, cruel Erisichthon, who not only defaced these holy trees, but also murdered this chaste nymph!"

Erisichthon said:

"Nymph, or goddess, it does not matter, for there is no one whom Erisichthon cares for, except Erisichthon.

"Let Ceres, the lady of your harvest, take revenge when she will — indeed, when she dares! And tell her this: that I am Erisichthon."

It is a mistake to offend the gods because the gods are powerful, and they will get revenge.

It is also a mistake to let offended gods know your name because the gods are not omniscient and if Ceres did not know who had cut down the tree and killed the nymph Fidelia, Ceres could not take revenge.

When Odysseus escaped from the cave of the one-eyed Cyclops Polyphemus after blinding his eye, he and his surviving men got on their ship and started to sail away. Odysseus, however, wanted Polyphemus to know who tricked and blinded him, and he yelled to the Cyclops, "Do you want to know who blinded you? It was I, Odysseus, son of Laertes. My home is Ithaca."

Immediately, Polyphemus prayed to his father, the god Poseidon, and asked for revenge against the Ithacan Odysseus, son of Laertes.

If Odysseus had not told the Cyclops his identity, the Cyclops would not have been able to pray to Poseidon and curse him. Poseidon may never have found out that it was Odysseus who blinded his son, Polyphemus, and he would not have known to hate Odysseus.

In this case the nymphs already knew Erisichthon's name. Still, his telling the nymphs to tell Ceres his name is an act of hubris: overweening pride.

"Thou are none of the gods," Niobe said to Erisichthon.

"No, I am a despiser and scorner of the gods," Erisichthon said.

"And do thou hope to escape revenge, being just a man?" Nisa asked.

"Yes, I don't worry about revenge, being a man and Erisichthon," he answered.

A proverb of the time stated, "Revenge is womanish."

Erisichthon exited.

Nisa said to the other nymphs:

"Come, let us go to Ceres, and complain about this unparalleled and not-to-be-believed villain: Erisichthon.

"If there is power in her deity, if there is pity in her mind, or if there is virtue in virginity, this monster cannot escape."

The three nymphs left to inform Ceres about the sacrilege Erisichthon had done to her sacred tree and to tell her about the death of Fidelia.

CHAPTER 2

— 2.1 —

At Ceres' tree, now felled, Ceres and the nymphs Niobe, Nisa, and Celia met.

Although the three nymphs all served Ceres, they were different:

Nisa believed that she could resist any man, and she did not believe in true love.

Celia wanted to stay beautiful and not have children.

Niobe did not want to have just one man.

Another nymph, who was named Tirtena, was present.

Ceres said:

"Does Erisichthon offer violence to my nymphs, and does he offer disgrace to my deity?

"Have I stuffed his barns with fruitful grain, and does he stretch his hand against me with intolerable pride?

"So it is, Ceres, thine eyes may witness what thy nymphs have told you; here lies the tree hacked in pieces, and here is the blood scarcely cold of the fairest virgin.

"If this is the result of thy cruelty, Cupid, I will no longer hallow and do reverence to thy temple with sacred vows."

Ceres thought that possibly, Cupid had inspired Erisichthon to do this evil deed.

Ceres continued:

"If this is the result of thy malignant, cankered nature, Erisichthon, thou shall find as great misery as thou have shown malice. I have decided on thy punishment, and as speedy shall be my revenge as thy cruelty has been barbarous."

She then ordered:

"Tirtena, on yonder hill, where neither grain nor leaf ever grew, where there is nothing except barrenness and coldness, fear and paleness, Famine lies.

"Go to her and say that Ceres commands her to gnaw on the bowels of Erisichthon, so that his hunger may be as unquenchable as is his fury."

"I obey," Tirtena said, "but how will I know Famine from others?"

Ceres answered:

"Thou cannot fail to recognize her, if thou just remember her name; and thou cannot forget her name because when thou come near to the place, thou shall find gnawing in thy stomach.

"She lies with open mouth, and swallows nothing except air.

"Her face is pale, and so lean, that thou may through the very skin behold the bone, as easily as in a mirror thou may behold thy reflection.

"Her hair is long, black, and shaggy.

"Her eyes are sunk so far into her head that she looks out of the back of her neck.

"Her lips are white and rough.

"Her teeth are hollow and red with rustiness: discoloration."

Her teeth are "rusty" because they have not been used.

Ceres continued:

"Her skin is so thin that thou may as clearly make an anatomy of and analyze her body, as if she were cut up by surgeons."

An anatomy is a skeleton.

Ceres continued:

"Her stomach is like a dry bladder.

"Her heart is swollen big with wind; and all her intestines are like snakes working in her body.

"This monster, when thou shall see her, tell her my instructions, and return with speed."

"I go, fearing more the sight of Famine than the force and effect of famine itself," Tirtena said.

"Take thou these few ears of corn, but do not let Famine so much as smell them; and let her go on the windward side from thee," Ceres said.

Tirtena could eat the corn to help avoid the effects of famine, but she needed to stand in such a way that the wind would not blow the scent of the corn to Famine.

Tirtena exited.

Ceres then said:

"Now shall Erisichthon see that Ceres is a great goddess, as full of power as he himself is full of pride, and he will see that Ceres is as pitiless as he is presumptuous.

"What do you think, ladies? Isn't this revenge apt punishment for so great an injury?"

"Yes, madam," Niobe said. "This punishment will let men see that they who contend with the gods only confound and ruin themselves."

Ceres said:

"But let us go to the temple of Cupid and make an offering.

"They who think it strange for chastity to humble itself to Cupid, know neither the power of love, nor the nature of virginity: Love has absolute authority to command, and so virgins find it difficult to resist love.

"Where such continual war is between love and virtue, there must be some parleys and continual perils."

Parleys are conversations between enemies; for example, a parley could be held when an army is besieging a castle. The besieging army may ask — or demand — that those in the castle surrender.

Ceres continued:

"Cupid has never been conquered, and therefore he must be flattered; virginity has been conquered, and therefore it must be humble."

"Into my heart, madam, there did never enter any motion or impulse of love," Nisa said.

Ceres said:

"Those who often say that they cannot love, or will not love, certainly they love."

Nisa believed that she could resist any man.

Ceres asked her:

"Have thou ever seen Cupid?"

Nisa replied:

"No, but I have heard him described fully, and, as I imagined, foolishly.

"First, he is described as a blind and naked god, with wings, with bow, with arrows, with firebrands, aka flaming torches; swimming sometimes in the sea, and playing sometimes on the shore; with many other attributes, which the painters, being the poets' apes — that is, imitators — have taken as great pains to paint, as the poets have taken great pains to lie.

"Can I think that gods who command all things would go naked?

"What should he do with wings who does not know where to fly?

"Or what should he do with arrows, who does not see how to aim? The heart is a narrow mark to hit, and rather requires Argus' eyes to take aim than a blind boy to shoot at random."

Argus was a giant with a hundred eyes.

Nisa continued:

"If he were fire, then the sea would quench those coals, or the flame would turn him into cinders."

"Well, Nisa, thou shall see him," Ceres said.

"I fear Niobe has felt his power," Nisa said,

Niobe, who did not want to be tied down to one lover, said:

"Not I, madam."

It sounds as if Niobe has had no lovers so far. She may have teased many men without having a relationship with any of them.

She continued:

"Yet I must confess that I have had often sweet thoughts, sometimes hard and hostile thoughts, and between both, I have had a kind of yielding.

"I don't know what it is.

"But certainly, I think it is not love.

"I can sigh and find ease and relief in feelings of melancholy.

"I smile, and I take pleasure in imagination.

"I feel in myself a pleasing pain, a chill heat, a delicate bitterness — I don't know what to call it. Without doubt it may be love; I am sure that it is not hate."

"Niobe is tender-hearted, and her thoughts are like water: yielding to everything, and nothing to be seen," Nisa said.

Ceres said:

"Well, let us go to Cupid.

"Take heed that in your stubbornness in refusing to love, you don't offend him, whom by entreaties you ought to follow: You should pray to him.

"Diana's nymphs were as chaste as Ceres' virgins, as fair, as wise. How Cupid tormented them, I had rather you should hear than feel, but this is the truth, they all yielded to love.

"Don't look so scornfully, my nymphs, I say they yielded to love."

Diana's Greek name is Artemis, and she is the virgin goddess of the hunt. Her nymphs were also virgins, and when Cupid pursued one of them and was rejected by her, he made Diana's nymphs fall in love with two girls who were disguised as boys. John Lyly tells this story in his play *Gallathea,* aka *Galathea.*

Ceres then said:

"This is Cupid's temple."

The temple doors opened, and Cupid came out.

Ceres said:

"Thou great god Cupid, whom the gods regard with respect, and men revere and worship, let it be lawful and permissible for Ceres to give her offering."

Cupid, who was a clothed handsome young man rather than a naked cherub, replied, "Divine Ceres, Cupid accepts anything that comes from Ceres, who feeds my sparrows with ripe corn, feeds my pigeons with wholesome seeds, and honors my temple with chaste virgins."

Despite all her talk about wanting many lovers, Niobe was a virgin.

Ceres, referring to Cupid as Love, said:

"Then, Love, to thee I bring these white and spotless and pure doves, in token that my heart is as free from any thought of love, as these are free from any blemish, and as clear in virginity, as these are perfect in whiteness."

She then said:

"But so that my nymphs may know both thy power and thy laws, and so that they will err neither in ignorance nor in pride, let me ask some questions to instruct them so that they will not offend thee, whom they cannot resist."

She then asked, "In virgins what do thou chiefly desire?"

"In those who are not in love, I chiefly desire reverent thoughts of love; in those who are in love, I chiefly desire faithful vows," Cupid said.

"What do thou most hate in virgins?" Ceres asked.

"Pride in the beautiful, bitter taunts in the witty, incredulity and disbelief in all," Cupid answered.

Celia was proud of her beauty.

Niobe teased the forester who loved her.

Nisa did not believe that she would ever fall in love.

"What may protect my virgins so that they may never love?" Ceres asked.

"That they never are idle," Cupid replied.

"Why did thou so cruelly torment all Diana's nymphs with love?" Ceres asked.

"Because they thought it impossible to love," Cupid replied.

"What is the substance — the essence — of love?" Ceres asked.

"Constancy and secrecy," Cupid replied.

"What are the physical signs of love?" Ceres asked.

"Sighs and tears," Cupid replied.

"What are the causes of love?" Ceres asked.

"Wit and idleness," Cupid replied.

"What are the means of love?" Ceres asked. "What means will a lover use?"

"Opportunity and importunity," Cupid replied.

"Importunity" means persistence.

"What is the end or goal of love?" Ceres asked.

"Happiness without end," Cupid replied.

"What do thou require from men?" Ceres asked.

"That shall be known by men only," Cupid replied. "I won't tell a woman that."

"What is your revenge for those who will not love?" Ceres asked.

"To be deceived by their lover when they do love," Cupid replied.

Ceres then said:

"Well, Cupid, treat my nymphs well, and though to love is no vice, yet spotless virginity is the only virtue.

"Let me keep their thoughts as chaste as their bodies, so that Ceres may be happy, and they may be praised."

Cupid said:

"Why, Ceres, do you think that lust follows love?

"Ceres, lovers are chaste: for what is love, divine love, but the quintessence of chastity, and affections binding by heavenly impulses, which cannot be undone by earthly means and must not be controlled by any man?"

Chasteness does not mean virginity, although all virgins are chaste. To be chaste is to be free from all *unlawful* sexual intercourse. A husband and a wife who sleep only with each other are chaste.

Chaste love — genuine and honorable love — between a husband and wife can include sex. Many religions say that it ought to include sex with some exceptions such as physical or mental disability that makes sex painful or impossible.

According to Judaism, chaste sex is a *mitzvah*.

A *mitzvah* is 1) a commandment, and 2) a good deed.

Ceres said:

"We will honor thee with continual sacrifice.

"Warm us with mild affections; lest being too hot, we seem immodest like wantons, or lest being too cold, we seem immoveable and incapable of feeling like stocks."

Stocks are tree trunks.

Ceres was seeking a mean between extremes: not too hot, like reckless lustfulness, nor too cold, like people who are frigid in sexual desire.

Cupid said:

"Ceres, let this advice serve for all.

"Don't let thy nymphs be light and easily won nor let them be obstinate; but let them be as virgins should be — compassionate and faithful.

"Do this so that your flames shall warm but shall not burn.

"And do this so that your flames shall delight and shall never cause discomfort and distress."

Cupid went into his temple.

Ceres said:

"What do you say, my nymphs? Doesn't Cupid speak like a god?

"I will not tell you to love, but I will implore you not to be disdainful of love.

"Let us go and see how Erisichthon is doing.

"Famine flies swiftly, and she has already seized on his stomach."

They exited.

CHAPTER 3

— 3.1 —

Ramis pursued Nisa in a glade in the forest.

Nisa believed that she could resist any man. She mocked love, and she did not believe that true love exists.

Ramis said:

"Stay, cruel Nisa, thou don't know from whom thou flee, and therefore thou flee.

"I don't come to offer violence, but instead to offer that which is inviolable: My thoughts are as holy as thy vows to remain chaste, and I am as constant and faithful in love as thou are in cruelty.

"Lust does not follow my love as shadows follow bodies, but truth is woven into my love, as veins are woven into bodies.

"Let me touch this tender arm of yours, and say my love is endless."

"And to no end," Nisa said.

"My love is without spot and sin," Ramis said.

"And shall be without hope," Nisa said.

"Do thou disdain Love and his laws?" Ramis asked.

Love is a name for Cupid, god of love.

"I do not disdain that which I think does not exist, yet I laugh at those who honor it as if it exists," Nisa said.

Nisa did not believe that true love exists.

"Time shall bring to pass that Nisa shall confess that there is love," Ramis said.

"Then love will also make me confess that Nisa is a fool," Nisa said.

"Is it folly to love, which the gods account as honorable, and men esteem as holy?" Ramis asked.

"The gods are capable of making anything lawful, because they are gods, and men honor shadows for substance, because they are men," Nisa said.

"Both gods and men agree that love is a consuming and a restoring of the heart, a bitter death in a sweet life," Ramis said.

Love can burn one's heart. It can bring both pain and pleasure.

"Gods know, and men should know, that love is a consuming of wit, and a restoring of folly; it is a staring blindness, and a blind gazing," Nisa said.

In other words: Love takes away a person's intelligence and makes them foolish. And people in love tend not to see anything but their beloved. Certainly, when first in love, they can think of little else but their beloved.

"Would thou allot me death?" Ramis asked.

"No, but I would allot you discretion," Nisa said.

"Yield to me some hope," Ramis requested.

"Hope to despair," Nisa said.

The word "hope" can mean "expect."

"I will not despair as long as Nisa is a woman," Ramis said.

"Therein, Ramis, you show yourself to be a man," Nisa said.

"Why?" Ramis asked.

"In flattering yourself that all women will yield," Nisa said.

"All may," Ramis said.

"Thou shall swear that we cannot," Nisa said.

In other words: Not all women will yield. They have a choice.

"I will follow thee, and I will practice by denials to be patient, or by disdaining I will die, and so be happy," Ramis said.

Ramis and Nisa exited, with Ramis running after Nisa.

Montanus and Celia entered the scene. Montanus was pursuing Celia.

Celia wanted to stay beautiful and not have children. She thought that she was above love.

"Though thou have overtaken me in love, yet I have overtaken thee in running," Montanus said. "Fair Celia, yield to love, to sweet love!"

Celia said:

"Montanus, thou are mad. Thou have almost no breath due to running so fast, yet thou will spend more breath in speaking so foolishly.

"Yield to love I cannot; or if I do, to thy love I will not."

Montanus replied:

"The fairest wolf chooses the ugliest male wolf, if he is the most faithful, and the fairest wolf chooses the wolf who endures the most grief.

"The fairest wolf does not choose the male wolf that has the most beauty.

"If my thoughts were wolvish, thy hopes might be as thy comparison is — beastly," Celia said.

"I wish that thy words were, as thy looks are, lovely," Montanus said.

"I wish thy looks were, as thy affection is — blind," Celia replied.

Montanus' "looks" were his sense of seeing.

"Fair faces should have smooth hearts," Montanus said.

"Fresh flowers have crooked roots," Celia said.

"Women's beauties will wane, and then no art can make them fair!" Montanus said.

Makeup can do only so much.

"Men's follies will forever wax and grow, and then what reason can make them wise?" Celia asked.

"To be amiable, and not to love, is like a painted lady: to have colors, and no life," Montanus said.

A painted lady is a woman wearing makeup, or a woman in a painting.

"To be amorous, and not lovely, is like a pleasant, merry fool, full of words, and no deserts — without merit," Celia said.

"What do you call you deserts, and what do you call lovely?" Montanus asked.

"There is no lovelier thing than wit, and there is no greater desert than patience," Celia said.

"Wit" is intelligence.

"Haven't I an excellent wit?" Montanus asked.

"If thou think so thyself, thou are an excellent fool," Celia said.

"Fool?" Montanus said. "No, Celia, thou shall find me as wise as I find thee proud; and as little to digest and tolerate thy taunts, as thou to brook and tolerate my love."

"I thought, Montanus, that you could not deserve, when I told you what desert was: patience," Celia said.

"Sweet Celia, I will be patient and forget this," Montanus said.

"Then you lack wit, if you can be content to be patient," Celia said.

Montanus said:

"That is a hard choice.

"If I take all well and have patience, then I lack wit and am a fool.

"But if find fault, then I lack patience and desert."

"The fortune of love, and the virtue, is to have neither success in love nor the means to acquire it," Celia said. "Farewell!"

Often, love is unrequited and so it is the fortune of love; however, the virtue of love is chasteness and loyalty in the sense that Cupid thinks of it: loving someone and being faithful to that person.

She ran away.

Montanus said:

"Farewell? Nay, I will follow!

"And I don't know how it comes to pass, but disdain increases desire; and the further away possibility stands, the nearer hope approaches.

"I now follow you!"

The more Nisa disdained and scorned him, the more he wanted her.

The more that it seemed that he would never have Nisa, the more he hoped to have her.

Montanus ran after Nisa.

Niobe ran onto the scene, closely followed by Silvestris.

Niobe did not want to have just one man. She hated the kind of love that leads to loyalty and chasteness.

"A polypus, Niobe, is always the color of the stone it sticks to; and thou are always of the mood of whatever man thou talk with," Silvestris said.

A polypus is a sea creature that can change its color.

Is Niobe "always of the mood of whatever man" she talks to? Not always. She does not match the mood of Silvestris.

"Do you find fault with me because I love?" Niobe asked.

"I find fault with thee because thou love so many," Silvestris said.

"Would you have me like no one?" Niobe asked.

"I would like thee to love one man," Silvestris said.

"Who shall make the choice of whom to love except myself?" Niobe asked.

"I myself," Silvestris said.

Niobe said:

"For another to put thoughts into my head would be to pull the brains out of my head. Don't take the measure of my affections but do weigh your own. Don't judge my love but do criticize your love.

"The oak finds no fault with the dew because the dew also falls on the bramble."

Niobe wanted to love many men, and she wanted Silvestris to be like the oak and not find fault.

Niobe continued:

"Believe me, Silvestris, the only way to be mad is to be constant and loyal to one person.

"Poets make their wreathes of laurel; ladies make their wreathes of several and various flowers."

Silvestris replied:

"Sweet Niobe, a river running into diverse brooks becomes shallow, and a mind divided into various affections will have none in the end.

"What joy can I take in the fortune of my love, when I shall know many to have the like favors?

"Turtledoves flock by couples and breed both joy and young ones."

Turtledoves mated for life. Silvestris wanted Niobe and him to mate for life.

"But bees flock in swarms, and bring forth wax and honey," Niobe said.

"Why do you covet many, when you may find sweetness in one?" Silvestris asked.

"Why did Argus have one hundred eyes, and might have seen with one?" Niobe asked.

"Because while he slept with some eyes, he might be awake with some other eyes," Silvestris said.

"And I love many because, being deceived by the inconstancy and disloyalty of various men, I might yet have one who is constant and loyal," Niobe said.

"That men are inconstant and disloyal is just an idea propagated by Juno, who knew that her husband, Jupiter, cheated on her," Silvestris said.

Jupiter was a notoriously unfaithful husband, and Juno was a notoriously jealous wife.

"And this is a rule of Venus, who knew men's lightness and promiscuity," Niobe said.

Possibly, Venus knew that men were promiscuous because she slept with so many gods and mortals.

"The whole heaven has only one sun," Silvestris said.

"But the heaven has an infinite number of stars," Niobe said.

"The rainbow is always in one circumference," Silvestris said.

"But the rainbow is made of various colors," Niobe said.

"A woman has but one heart," Silvestris said.

"But a woman has a thousand thoughts," Niobe said.

"My lute, although it has many strings, makes a sweet consent — a sweet harmony — and a lady's heart, although it harbors many fancies, should embrace only one love," Silvestris said.

"The strings of my heart are tuned in a contrary key to your lute and make as sweet harmony in discords as yours make in concord," Niobe said.

"Why, what strings are in ladies' hearts?" Silvestris said. "Not the bass."

The bass string produces a low note.

"There is no base string in a woman's heart," Niobe said.

"The mean?" Silvestris asked.

The mean string produces an intermediate note.

"There was never mean in a woman's heart," Niobe said.

"The treble string?"

The treble string produces a high note.

"Yea, the treble double and treble — double and triple," Niobe said, "and so are all my heartstrings. Farewell!"

The treble is the highest part in a song for three voices.

Niobe wanted to double and triple the number of her lovers.

"Sweet Niobe, let us sing, so that I may die with the swan," Silvestris said.

Swans were reputed to sing before they died.

"It will make you sigh the more, and live with the salamich," Niobe said.

The salamich is the salamander, which was reputed to be able to live in fire.

"Are thy tunes fire?" Silvestris asked.

"Are your tunes death?" Niobe asked.

"No, but after I have heard thy voice, I am content to die," Silvestris said.

"I will sing to content thee," Niobe said.

Hmm. Sing to make thee happy? Or sing to make thee happy to die?

She sang, and then she exited.

Silvestris did not die. He also was not made happy.

He said, "Inconstant Niobe! Unhappy Silvestris! Yet I prefer that she should love all rather than none, for now although I have no certainty, yet I find a kind of sweetness."

If Niobe loved all, then Silvestris would have a share of her love. If Niobe loved none, then Silvestris would not have a share of her love.

Ramis returned to the scene and said, "Cruel Nisa, born to slaughter men!"

Montanus returned to the scene and said, "Coy Celia, bred up in scoffs!"

Silvestris said:

"Wavering, yet witty Niobe!"

The word "witty" means "intelligent."

Silvestris then asked:

"But are we all met?"

Ramis replied, "Yes, and we have met our matches, if your fortunes are similar to mine, for I find my mistress immoveable, and the only hope I have is to despair."

His "mistress" was the nymph whom he loved.

"My mistress is intolerable in pride, and she orders me to look for no other comfort than her contempt and scorn," Montanus said.

"My mistress is best of all, and worst of all," Silvestris said. "This is my hope, that either she will have many lovers or none."

If she has no lovers, Silvestris will not be jealous of them; if she has many lovers, Silvestris may be one of them, and he will have a share of her love. Niobe had given him no hope that she would have one lover.

Ramis said:

"I fear our fortunes cannot thrive, for Erisichthon has felled the holy tree of Ceres, which will increase her anger, and which will increase cruelty in her nymphs.

"Let us see whether our garlands that we hanged on that tree are still there; and let us hang ourselves upon another tree."

Unrequited lovers sometimes hung themselves — or threatened to hang themselves.

Silvestris said:

"Hanging is a remedy for love that is inflexible and unmovable, but I will first see whether all those who love Niobe do likewise.

"In the meantime, I will content myself with my share."

Silvestris did not want to hang himself if Niobe's other lovers had not.

Montanus said:

"Here is the tree.

"O, mischief scarcely to be believed, impossible to be pardoned!"

Ramis said:

"Pardoned it is not, for Erisichthon perishes with famine, and he is able to starve those who look at him.

"Here our garlands hang.

"Something is written; read mine."

Silvestris read, "*Cedit amor rebus, res age, tutus eris.*"

Translated, the quotation says, "Love gives way to things, keep busy, you will be safe."

In other words: Keep busy, and you can avoid falling in love.

Montanus said, "And read mine."

Silvestris read:

"*Sat mihi si facies, sit bene nota mihi.*"

Translated, the Latin means, "If you will pursue me, let it be well known to me."

One way for Montanus to do that would be to praise Celia's beauty.

Silvestris then said:

"Now for myself: *Victoria tecum stabit.*"

Translated, the quotation says, "Victory rests with you."

He then said:

"*Scilicet.*"

This Latin word means, "Indeed" or "Of course."

He had read the motto that Niobe had written, but that didn't mean he believed it.

Montanus said:

"You see their posies are like their hearts; and their hearts are like their speeches — cruel, proud, and wavering."

Nisa was cruel.

Celia was proud of her beauty.

Niobe was wavering and fickle in her love.

"Let us all go to the temple of Cupid, and entreat and beg for his favor, if not to obtain their loves, yet to revenge their hates: Cupid is a kind god who, knowing our unspotted thoughts and love for the nymphs, will punish them or release us."

Cupid had arrows made of lead as well as arrows made of gold.

When he shot an arrow made of lead at someone, that person's love would change to hate.

When he shot an arrow made of gold at someone, that person would fall in love.

Montanus continued:

"We will study what revenge to have, so that, our pains proceeding of our own minds, their plagues may also proceed from theirs.

"Are you all agreed?"

"I agree, but what if Cupid denies us his help?" Silvestris asked.

"Then he is no god," Montanus said.

"But if he yields to our entreaties and will help us, what shall we ask for?" Silvestris asked.

"Revenge," Ramis said.

"Then let us prepare ourselves for Cupid's sacrifice," Montanus said.

— **3.2** —

On the seashore near Erisichthon's farm, Erisichthon and Protea, his daughter, talked.

Erisichthon said:

"Come, Protea, dear daughter. That name of 'daughter of Erisichthon' thou must buy too expensively. Necessity causes thee to be sold; nature must frame thee to be contented."

In other words: Her filial love for her father must make her consent to being sold.

Erisichthon continued:

"Thou see in how short a time I have turned all my goods into my guts, where I feel a continual fire that nothing can quench. My famine increases by eating, resembling the sea, which receives all things, and cannot be filled."

Erisichthon had sold his land and possessions so he could buy food, but eating did not stop his hunger — it only increased it.

Now all he had left to sell was his daughter: Protea.

Erisichthon continued:

"Life is sweet, and hunger is sharp. Between them the contention must be short, unless thou, Protea, prolong it.

"I have acknowledged my offence against Ceres; but I cannot make amends, for the gods hold the balance in their hands, and so what recompence can equally weigh with their punishments?

"Or who is he who, having but one ill thought of Ceres, can erase it with a thousand dutiful actions?

"Such is the difference that none can find defense. This is the difference: We are miserable, and men; they are immortal, and gods."

The gods and goddesses can be unforgiving for trivial offenses as well as for great offenses.

Erisichthon has already repented cutting down Ceres' tree, but Ceres has not forgiven him. He is still being tormented by Famine.

Protea responded:

"Dear father, I will obey and consent both to sale and slaughter, considering it the only happiness of my life, if I should I live a hundred years, to prolong your life just one minute."

"Sale and slaughter" referred to market animals. Protea would be sold and would become a slave, but she would not be slaughtered for meat.

Protea continued:

"I yield, father: Chop and change me."

"Chop and change me" meant "Barter away. Make the bargain."

Protea continued:

"I am ready; but first let me make my prayers to Neptune, and you withdraw yourself until I have finished. It shall not be long, but it must be now."

Neptune is the god of the sea.

Protea wanted her father to step away so he would not hear her prayer to Neptune.

"Stay, sweet Protea, and may that great god hear thy prayer, although Ceres stops her ears to mine," Erisichthon said.

Erisichthon stepped away.

Protea prayed:

"Sacred Neptune, whose godhead conquered my virginity and maidenhead, be as ready to hear my passions, as I was to believe thine, and perform that which now I entreat you for, which thou did promise when thyself did love."

The gods often sleep with mortals, and Neptune had slept with Protea after promising to help her if she ever needed help.

Protea continued:

"Don't allow me to be a prey to this merchant who knows no other god than gold unless it be falsely swearing by a god to get gold.

"Do let me, as often as I am bought for money, or pawned for meat and food, be turned into a bird, hare, or lamb, or any shape in which I may be safe, as long as I shall preserve my own honor, preserve my father's life, and never repent of thy love."

Protea wanted to become a shape-shifter so she could escape from whoever bought her. The merchant would buy her, pay her father money, and then Protea would change her shape and escape.

In Homer's *Odyssey*, a minor sea-god named Proteus is a shape-shifter. Menelaus encountered him and learned information about Odysseus' location and about Menelaus' own return home.

Protea continued:

"And now bestir thee, for of all men I hate that merchant, who, if he finds my beauty worth one penny, will put it to use to gain ten; he has no religion in his mind, nor word in his mouth, except money."

One way to put Protea's beauty to use would be to prostitute her.

Protea continued:

"Neptune, hear me now or never."

She then said, "Father, I have finished praying."

Stepping forward, Erisichthon said, "In good time, Protea. Thou have finished at a good time, for look, the merchant keeps not only the day, but the hour."

The merchant was coming toward them at the exact time appointed.

"If I had not been here, would I have been forfeited?" Protea asked. "Would I have been sold?"

"No, Protea, but thy father would have famished and starved to death," Erisichthon said.

Protea would not have been sold, and her father would not have received any money with which to buy food.

The merchant entered the scene.

"Here, gentleman, I am ready with my daughter," Erisichthon said.

"Gentleman?" Protea asked.

The word "gentleman" can refer to 1) good character, or to 2) social position and wealth.

A gentleman of good character is a person who exhibits good and courteous behavior. A gentleman does not buy women.

A gentleman of social position and wealth is a man of the lowest rank of the English aristocracy. He can bear arms, but he has no title.

"Yes, gentleman, fair maiden!" the merchant said. "My financial circumstances make me no less than a gentleman."

"Your financial circumstances indeed brought in your obligations, your obligations your usury, and your usury your gentry," Protea said.

The merchant was a merchant of money: a usurer.

His wealth brought in his financial contracts (loans to others), which brought in more wealth through interest, which allowed him to purchase the name of gentleman.

"Why, do you judge no merchants to be gentlemen?" the merchant asked.

"Yes, I judge many merchants to be gentlemen, and I judge some merchants to be no men!" Protea said.

If they are not men, then they are beasts.

"You shall be well entreated at my hands," the merchant said.

"Entreated" means 1) begged or pleaded with, or 2) treated.

"Maybe," Protea said. "I will not be commanded."

"If you are mine by bargain, you shall be commanded," the merchant said. "You will have to do what I tell you to do."

Protea asked, "Father, has this merchant also bought my mind?"

"He cannot buy that which cannot be sold," Erisichthon answered.

"Here is the money," the merchant said, handing it over.

Erisichthon said to the merchant:

"Here is the maiden."

He then said to Protea, "Farewell, my sweet daughter; I commit thee to the gods and this man's courtesy, who I hope will deal no worse with thee than he would have the gods deal with him."

In other words: I hope that the merchant will treat you the way that he hopes the gods would treat him.

Erisichthon then said:

"I must be gone, lest I starve as I stand here."

"Farewell, dear father, I will not cease to pray to Ceres continually for thy recovery," Protea said.

Erisichthon exited.

"You are now mine, Protea," the merchant said.

"And I am my own," Protea said.

"In will, not power," the merchant said.

"In power if I will," Protea said.

"I perceive that nettles, gently touched, sting; but, when they are roughly handled, they cause no pain," the merchant said.

A proverb stated that "he which touchest the nettle tenderly is soonest stung."

The meaning of the proverb is "Face danger bravely and it won't hurt you."

Aaron Hill (1685-1750) wrote:

Tender-handed stroke a nettle,
And it stings you for your pains;
Grasp it like a man of mettle,
And it soft as silk remains.
'Tis the same with common natures,
Use [Treat] them kindly they rebel;
But be rough as nutmeg graters,
And the rogues obey you well.

"Yet, roughly handled, nettles are nettles, and a wasp is a wasp, although she loses her sting," Protea said.

"But then they do no harm," the merchant said.

"Nor good," Protea said.

"Come with me, and you shall see that merchants know their good as well as gentlemen," the merchant said.

"I am sure that they have gentlemen's goods," Protea said.

When gentlemen could not pay their debts, usurers would foreclose on the debts, taking whatever the gentlemen had pledged as security.

CHAPTER 4

— 4.1 —

The three foresters — Ramis, Montanus, and Silvestris — stood before the temple of Cupid. Ramis held burning lamps, Montanus held a distaff (used in spinning thread and yarn) and a noose, and Silvestris held a fan made of feathers and a garland made of flowers. These were offerings to Cupid. Each of them would also offer a metaphorical picture of his heart to Cupid. Ramis' heart was bleeding, Montanus' heart was bloodless, and Silvestris' heart was swollen.

"This is the temple of our great god," Ramis said. "Let us offer our sacrifice."

"I am ready," Montanus said.

Silvestris said:

"And I am ready."

He prayed:

"Cupid, thou god of love, whose arrows have pierced our hearts, give ear to our complaints."

The temple doors opened.

Cupid came out and said, "If you come to Cupid, speak boldly, so must lovers; speak faithfully, so must speeders."

"Speeders" are those who succeed.

Ramis said:

"These ever-burning lamps are signs of my never-to-be-quenched flames; this bleeding heart, in which yet sticks the head of the golden shaft, is the lively picture of inward torments.

"My eyes shall bedew thine altars with tears, and my sighs shall cover thy temple with a dark smoke.

"Pity poor Ramis."

Montanus said:

"With this distaff have I spun, so that my exercises may be as womanish as my affections, and so did Hercules."

As the result of some evil that Hercules had done, he became a slave to Omphale, the Queen of Lydia. She wore his lionskin, and Hercules dressed in women's clothing and did "women's work," such as spinning fibers into thread or yarn.

Montanus continued:

"And with this noose I will hang myself, if my fortunes don't answer my deserts, and so did Iphis."

A shepherd named Iphis fell in love with a proud woman named Anaxarete who scorned his advances, and he hung himself on her doorstep.

Montanus continued:

"To thee, divine Cupid, I present not a bleeding heart, but a bloodless heart, dried only with sorrow, and worn with faithful service.

"This picture I offer, carved with no other instrument than love.

"Pity poor Montanus."

Silvestris said:

"This fan of swans' and turtledoves' feathers is token of my truth and jealousy."

Swans and turtledoves were reputed to find mates for life.

Silvestris continued:

"Without jealousy, love is infatuation, and with jealousy, love is madness.

"Without jealousy, love is lust, and with jealousy, love is folly."

According to the *Oxford English Dictionary*, at the time John Lyly was writing, "jealousy" meant:

1) "Zeal or vehemence of feeling in favour of a person or thing; devotion, eagerness, anxiety to serve."

2) "Zeal or vehemence of feeling against some person or thing; anger, wrath, indignation."

The independent clauses using the phrase "Without jealousy" use the word "jealousy" with the first meaning.

The independent clauses using the phrase "with jealousy" use the word "jealousy" with the second meaning.

Silvestris continued:

"This heart, neither bleeding nor bloodless, but swollen with sighs, I offer to thy godhead, professing that all my thoughts are, as are my words, without lust, and all my love is, as is my fortune, without sweetness.

"This garland of flowers, which has all colors of the rainbow, witnesses that my heart has all the torments of the world.

"Pity poor Silvestris."

Cupid said, "I accept your offerings, not without reason; and I marvel at your loves, not without pleasure, but are your thoughts as true as your words?"

Ramis said, "Thou, Cupid, who gives the wound, knows the heart; for it is as impossible to conceal our affections, as it is to resist thy power."

Cupid said:

"I know that where my arrow alights, there love breeds; but shooting every minute a thousand shafts, I don't know on whose heart they alight, although they fall on no place but hearts.

"Who are your mistresses? Who are the women you love?"

Ramis said, "We love Ceres' maidens. Mine is the cruelest, which she calls 'constancy.'"

Maidens are virgins. If Niobe is a virgin, she talks a good game but does not actually play the game.

Nisa constantly believed that true love does not exist.

"Mine is the most beautiful, but she is also the proudest," Montanus said.

Celia wanted to stay beautiful and not have children.

"Mine is the wittiest, but she is also the most wavering," Silvestris said.

Niobe did not want to have just one man. She hated the kind of love that leads to loyalty and chasteness.

Cupid asked, "Is the one cruel, the next coy, and the third inconstant?"

"Too cruel!" Ramis said.

"Too coy!" Montanus said.

"Too fickle!" Silvestris said.

Cupid then asked, "What do they think of Cupid?"

"One says that Cupid has no eyes because he does not know whom he hits with his arrows," Ramis said.

So many people fall in love that Cupid must shoot very rapidly with the result that some people fall in love with someone who is clearly not suitable for them.

"The next says that Cupid has no ears that he could use to hear those who call on him," Montanus said.

"The third says that Cupid has no nose because savors are not found of lovers," Sylvestris said.

People can be so much in love that they forget to eat, especially when their love is unrequited, and they are grieving.

The sense of smell is related to the sense of taste. If you can't smell good food, it will not taste good or at least it will not taste as good as it would if you could smell it.

Niobe wanted to have many lovers. This is analogous to having a plate loaded with many kinds of food.

According to *the Oxford English Dictionary*, the noun "savour" or "savor" can mean "Pleasing, enjoyable, or attractive quality; merit, value."

The arrows that Cupid shoots tend to make one person fall in love with another person. According to Niobe, those monogamous lovers are missing out.

Woody Allen once said, "I believe that sex is a beautiful thing between two people. Between five, it's fantastic."

"All say that Cupid has no taste because sweet and sour is all one to him," Ramis said.

Cupid shoots many gold arrows, and the people he shoots fall in love. Sometimes the love is requited, and it is sweet, but sometimes the love is unrequited, and it is sour.

"All say that Cupid has no ability to feel because pains are pleasures, and pleasures are pains," Montanus said.

Falling in love can be pleasurable but can also lead to heartbreak.

"All say that Cupid is a foolish god, working without reason, and without regard allowing the rejected lovers to suffer the repulse," Silvestris said.

Love may not be rational, but it is not irrational. Love is nonrational.

Some things are rational, such as mathematics and logic. Other things are irrational, such as putting your hand in a blender and turning it on just to see what it feels like. The realm of the nonrational is the realm of beauty, poetry, laughter, dance, sex, and love. Comedy is nonrational. The arts connect the world of the rational and the nonrational. Much intelligence goes into producing art, but much art explores the world of the nonrational.

Love is nonrational. Suppose you are confronted with two individuals who are basically alike in beauty, form, character, and personality, but one individual is rich and the other individual is poor. Reason would tell you to fall in love with the rich individual, but you may fall in love with the poor individual.

Cupid replied:

"Do they dare to blaspheme my godhead, which Jove worships, Neptune revers, and all the gods tremble at?"

All the gods were afraid of Cupid because he could make them fall in love. Jupiter, aka Jove, had a jealous wife who hated the women he had sex with.

Cupid continued:

"To make the nymphs love would be a revenge too gentle for Cupid.

"To make you hate the nymphs would be a recompense too small for lovers.

"But I'll say more about that soon.

"Right now, tell me what tactics you have used in love to attract the nymphs."

"All things that may procure love — gifts, words and vows, oaths and promises, and sighs and swoonings," Ramis said.

Swoonings are fainting fits.

"What did they say about the gifts?" Cupid asked.

"That affection could not be bought with gold," Montanus said.

"What did they say about the words and vows?" Cupid asked.

"That they were golden blasts, out of leaden bellows," Ramis said.

"What did they say about the oaths and promises?" Cupid asked.

"That Jupiter never swore true to Juno," Silvestris said.

Jupiter was a notoriously unfaithful husband who committed adultery with many mortal women and many immortal goddesses. Juno was his jealous wife.

"What did they say about sighs?" Cupid asked.

"That deceit kept a forge in the hearts of fools," Silvestris said.

The nymphs believed or said that they believed that the foresters were fools, and therefore the foresters' hearts and sighs were deceitful.

Cupid, however, is likely to regard the nymphs as fools for not yielding to love.

"What did they say about the swoonings?" Cupid asked.

"Nothing, except that they wished the swoonings were deaths," Montanus said.

"What reasons did they give for them not to love?" Cupid asked.

"Women's reasons," Silvestris said. "They would not, because they would not."

In other words, each nymph's excuse was this: Because I said so.

Cupid said:

"Well, then shall you see Cupid repay their reasons with his harshness.

"What punishment do you desire that Cupid will deny?"

Cupid intended to grant whatever *reasonable* punishment the foresters asked for. If they asked for something *unreasonable*, he would deny that punishment.

Ramis said, "Mine, who is as hard as stone, I would have turned into stone. She has been pitiless to lovers, so now let she be without the physical senses to all the world."

Montanus said, "Mine, who is so fair and so proud, I would have turned into some flower so that she may know beauty is as fading as grass, which, being fresh in the morning, has withered before night."

Silvestris said, "Divine Cupid, let mine, whose affection nothing can make constant, be turned into that bird that lives only by air, and dies if she touches the earth, because it is constant. Turn her into the bird-of-paradise, Cupid, so that, drawing into her bowels nothing but air, she may know that her heart is fed on nothing but fickleness."

The bird-of-paradise was reputed never to land on the earth and never to eat.

Cupid said:

"Your revenges are reasonable and shall be granted.

"Thou, **Nisa**, whose heart no tears could pierce, shall with continual waves be worn away.

"Instead of thy fair hair, thou shall have green moss.

"Thy face shall be of flint because thy heart is of marble. "Thine ears shall be holes for fishes because your ears were deafer than fishes' ears."

Nisa would be a rock on the beach.

Cupid continued:

"Thou, **Celia**, whom beauty made proud, shall have the fruit of beauty, that is, to fade while it is flourishing, and to wither before it is fully bloomed.

"Thy face, as fair as the damask rose, shall perish like the damask rose.

"The canker shall eat thee in the bud, and every little wind shall blow thee from the stalk, and then men in the morning shall wear thee in their hats, and at night they shall cast thee at their heels."

Celia would be a rose.

Cupid continued:

"Thou, **Niobe**, whom nothing can please (except that which most displeases Cupid, inconstancy), shall only breathe and suck air instead of food, and wear feathers instead of silk, being more wavering and fickler than air, and lighter than feathers."

Niobe would be a bird.

"Lighter" can mean 1) less heavy, and 2) more promiscuous.

Cupid said:

"This will Cupid do.

"Therefore, when next you shall behold your ladies, just send a faithful sigh to Cupid, and there shall arise a thick mist that Proserpine shall send, and at that moment you shall be revenged, and with the nymphs changed and metamorphosed, Cupid will prove that he is a great god, and that the nymphs are peevish, foolish girls."

Proserpine's mother is Ceres, goddess of agriculture. Pluto, the god of the Land of the Dead, kidnapped Proserpine and made her his wife. Ceres mourned and searched for her daughter, and while she mourned, no crops grew. Jupiter sent the messenger god Mercury to Pluto to make him allow Proserpine to go back to the Land of the Living. But Proserpine had eaten some pomegranate seeds and those who eat in the Land of the Dead were not supposed to go back to the Land of the Living. But since Proserpine had eaten so little, and since Jupiter did not want life on Earth to end, a compromise was reached. Proserpine would spend six months of the year in the Land of the Living and the other six months in the Land of the Dead.

When Proserpine is in the Land of the Living, Ceres is happy and crops grow, but when Proserpine is in the Land of the Dead, Ceres is unhappy, and crops don't grow.

Proserpine's Greek name is Persephone, and Ceres' Greek name is Demeter.

Jupiter's Greek name is Zeus, Pluto's Greek name is Hades, and Mercury's Greek name is Hermes.

"With what sacrifice shall we show that we are thankful, or how may we repay to you this benefit?" Ramis asked.

Cupid replied:

"You shall yearly at my temple offer true hearts, and hourly you shall bestow all your wits in loving devices."

"Loving devices" are inventive ways of showing love.

Cupid continued:

"You shall think all the time that is not spent in love is wasted.

"You shall let your oaths be without number, but not without truth.

"Your words shall be full of alluring sweetness, but not of broad and obvious flattery.

"Your clothing shall be neat, but not womanish.

"Your gifts shall be of more price for the fine device, than the great value, and yet of such value that the device shall seem not beggarly, nor yourselves blockish and stupid."

These devices are ways of showing love.

The gifts need not be expensive, but they should be carefully and thoughtfully chosen. Don't buy your beloved something that you like but your beloved doesn't.

Cupid continued:

"You shall be secret; secrecy works miracles.

"You shall be constant and loyal — that brings secrecy.

"This is all Cupid commands.

"Leave now!"

Ramis said, "And to this we all willingly consent."

The temple doors closed.

Silvestris said, "Now what remains to be done but revenge on them who have committed malice against us? Let mine be anything, seeing that she will not be only mine."

Montanus said, "Let us not now stand wishing, but immediately seek them out, using as great speed in following revenge as we did in pursuing our love; certainly, we shall find them around Ceres' tree, singing or sacrificing."

"But shall we go visit Erisichthon?" Silvestris asked.

Montanus said:

"Not I, lest he, who devours all things, eats us; his looks have the power to famish.

"Let us go in, and let all ladies beware to offend in spite those who love them in honor; for when the crow shall set his foot in their eye and create crow's feet, aka wrinkles, and the black ox tread on their foot and make it hurt, they shall find their misfortunes to be equal with their deformities, and men both to loath them and laugh at them."

Erisichthon and Protea stood together on the seashore near Erisichthon's farm.

"Come, Protea, tell me how did thou escape from the merchant?" Erisichthon asked.

Protea said:

"Neptune, that great god of the sea, when I was ready to go with the merchant into the ship, turned me into a fisherman on the shore, with a fishing pole in my hand, and on my shoulder a net.

"The merchant missing me, and yet finding me without recognizing me, asked me who I was, and whether I had seen a fair maiden?

"I answered, no!

"He, astonished and raging, was forced either to lose his passage, or seek for me among the pebbles! To make short a long story, a good wind caused him to go I don't know where, and me (thanks be to Neptune) to return home."

"Thou are happy, Protea, although thy father is miserable, and Neptune is gracious, although Ceres is cruel," Erisichthon said. "Thy escape from the merchant breeds in me life, joy, and fulfillment."

Protea said:

"My father cannot be miserable, if Protea is happy; for by selling me every day, he shall never lack food, nor shall I lack the means to escape.

"And now, father, give me permission to enjoy my Petulius, who on this unfortunate shore still seeks me sorrowing."

She wanted to spend some time with her boyfriend.

"Seek him, dear Protea; find and enjoy him, and live ever hereafter to thine own comforts, who have hitherto been the preserver of mine," Erisichthon said.

Protea wanted both to have a relationship with her boyfriend and to allow herself to be sold over and over again so that her father could have food.

Erisichthon exited.

"Oh!" Protea said. "Look, a Siren haunts this shore! May the gods forbid that she should entangle my Petulius."

The Siren was sitting on a rock. She did not notice Protea.

Sirens are part-woman. According to Apollonius of Rhodes, author of the *Argonautica*, an epic poem about Jason and the Argonauts, Sirens are part-bird.

Sirens sing beautiful songs to lure sailors to their deaths. The sailors hear the Sirens' song and jump overboard to swim to the Sirens. The sailors forget about their homecoming and instead stay with the Sirens and listen to their songs while forgetting to eat and slowly starving to death.

This Siren, however, resembled a mermaid.

In the Middle Ages, Sirens and mermaids became conflated.

Now, when we think of a Siren, we think of a beautiful mermaid who sings beautifully.

And when we think of a siren (with a small s), we think of a beautiful woman.

The Siren said, "Accursed men! Men's loves have no other mean than extremities, and their hates end in nothing but evil."

In other words: When men love, they use extreme means (such as deceit) to get what they want, and when men hate, their hatred brings evil to those whom they hate.

Protea said to herself, "Unnatural monster! She is no maid, who accuses men, whose loves are built on truths, and whose hearts are moved by courtesy. I will hear the depth of her malice."

The experience of Protea and the experience of the Siren with men was much different. Protea was happy with her relationship with her boyfriend, but the Siren's heart had been broken.

The Siren said:

"Men are of all creatures most unkind, most cunning.

"By men's subtleties, I am half fish, half flesh.

"Men themselves are neither fish nor flesh."

The expression "neither fish nor flesh" means "neither one nor the other." Men are not "flesh" because, according to the Siren, they don't act the right way toward her.

The Siren continued:

"In love men are lukewarm, and in cruelty they are red hot.

"If men praise, they flatter; if men flatter, they deceive; if men deceive, they destroy."

Protea said to herself:

"She rails at men, but she seeks to entangle them.

"This trick is prepared for my sweet Petulius.

"I will withdraw myself nearby, for Petulius has seen me and is following me and will come here.

"He will without doubt be enamored of her; but he shall not be enchanted — my charms shall countervail hers.

"Petulius has saved my father's life with money, and he must prolong my life with love."

Petulius had given Erisichthon money so he could buy food.

Petulius entered the scene and said:

"I marvel that Protea is so far ahead of me: If she runs, I'll fly."

He called:

"Sweet Protea, where are thou? It is Petulius who calls Protea."

The Siren said:

"Here comes a handsome youth.

"Now, Siren, leave out nothing that may allure — thy golden locks of hair, thy enticing looks, thy musically tuned voice, thy subtle speech, thy fair promises, which never missed the heart of any but Ulysses."

Ulysses' Greek name is Odysseus. In Homer's *Odyssey*, Odysseus' ship sailed by the Sirens. Ulysses wanted to hear the Sirens' song, so he ordered his men to tie him to the mast so he could not jump overboard. His men put beeswax in their ears so they could not hear the Sirens' song, and they rowed past the Sirens.

Another man who heard the Sirens' song but lived was Butes, a sharp-eared Argonaut. When Jason's ship, the *Argo*, sailed past the Sirens, Orpheus played his lyre loudly to drown out their song, but Butes' hearing was so sharp that he heard the Sirens' song and jumped overboard. Fortunately, the goddess Aphrodite felt pity for him and rescued him and set him on shore far from the Sirens.

The Siren sang, holding a mirror and a hair comb in her hand.

Petulius, reacting the way that other men had reacted, said:

"What divine goddess is this? What sweet harmony! My heart is ravished with such tickling thoughts, and my eyes stayed with such a bewitching beauty, that I can neither find the means to remove my affection and stop myself from falling in love, nor can I turn aside my eyes and not look at her."

The Siren sang again.

Petulius said to the Siren:

"I yield to death, but with such delight, that I would not wish to live, unless it were to hear thy sweet songs."

The Siren replied:

"Live always, as long as thou love me!

"Why do thou stand amazed at the word 'love'?"

This Siren seemed more like a heartbroken woman seeking love than a monster seeking to destroy sailors. Still, she was attempting to take Petulius away from Protea.

Protea, from her hiding place behind them, said to herself:

"It is high time to prevent this evil."

She prayed:

"Now, Neptune, stand to and keep thy promise, and let me take suddenly the shape of an old man; in that shape I shall mar what she makes."

Protea exited.

Petulius said:

"I have not yet come to myself, or if I have, I dare not credit my ears.

"Love thee, divine goddess?

"Grant to me that I may honor thee and live by the imagination I have of thy words and worthiness."

The Siren said, "I am a goddess, but I am also a lady and a virgin, whose love if thou embrace, thou shall live no less happy than the gods in heaven."

Protea reentered the scene. She had assumed the shape and appearance of an old man.

The metamorphosed Protea said, "Don't believe this enchantress, sweet youth. She retains the face of a virgin, but the heart of a fiend, whose sweet tongue sheds more drops of blood than it utters syllables."

Petulius said to the old man (the metamorphosed Protea), "Go away, dotterel! Your dim eyes cannot recognize beauty, nor can doting age judge of love."

He was calling her a dotard.

A dotterel is a senile old man. The word "dotterel" also referred to a bird that was easily caught and therefore thought to be stupid.

"If thou listen to her words, thou shall not live to repent," the old man (the metamorphosed Protea) said, "for her malice is as sudden as her joys are sweet."

"Thy silver hairs are not as precious as her golden locks, nor is thy crooked old age as esteemed as her flowering youth," Petulius said.

"That old man measures the hot assault of love with the cold skirmishes of age," the Siren said.

The old man (the metamorphosed Protea) said:

"That young cruel one — the Siren — resembles old apes, who kill by culling."

"Culling" means "hugging." Old apes, by showing excessive love to their young, end up killing them. So said the old man (the metamorphosed Protea).

The old man (the metamorphosed Protea) continued:

"From the top of this rock on which she is sitting, she will throw thee headlong into the sea.

"Her song is the instrument of her witchcraft.

"She never smiles except when she intends to smite, and under the flattery of love she practices the shedding of blood."

"Who are thou, who so blasphemes this divine creature?" Pentulius asked.

The old man (the metamorphosed Protea) said:

"I am the ghost of Ulysses, who continually hovers about these places where this Siren haunts, to save those who otherwise should be spoiled: stop thine ears, as I did mine, and succor and help the fair, but, by thy folly, the most unfortunate Protea."

Protea's reference to the myth of Ulysses (his Greek name is Odysseus) was incorrect. It was Ulysses' (Odysseus') men who had stopped their ears with beeswax.

"Protea?" Petulius said, recovering from the Siren's spell. "What do thou hear, Petulius? Where is Protea?"

The old man (the metamorphosed Protea) said:

"In this thicket, ready to hang herself because thou don't care for her whom thou did swear to follow.

"Curse this hag, who has only the voice and face of a virgin; the rest is all fish and feathers and filth. Follow me, and strongly stop thine ears, lest the second encounter make the wound incurable."

The Siren has feathers, so she may also be part-bird, unless she is wearing the feathers.

"Is this a Siren, and are thou Ulysses?" Petulius said. "Cursed be that hellish carcass, and blessed be thy heavenly spirit."

The Siren said:

"I shrink my head for shame.

"O, Ulysses! Isn't it enough for thee to escape from me, but must thou also teach others how to escape from me?"

She then said to herself:

"Sing and die, nay die, and never sing anymore."

The Siren exited.

The old man (the metamorphosed Protea) said to Petulius, "Follow me at this door, and then come out at the other door."

Of course, she was referring to stage doors.

The two exited, and then returned to the stage. Protea was now in her own shape.

"How I am delivered!" Petulius said. "The old man has vanished, and here in his place stands Protea."

Protea said:

"Here stands Protea, who has saved thy life.

"Thou must also prolong hers with love, but let us go into the woods, and there I will tell thee how I came to be Ulysses, and I will tell thee the sum of all my fortunes, which perhaps will breed in thee both love and wonder."

Petulius said, "I will, and I will love only Protea, and never cease to marvel at Protea."

They exited.

CHAPTER 5

— 5.1 —

In front of the temple of Cupid, Ceres and Cupid talked. The nymph Tirtena was also present.

Ceres said, "Cupid, thou have transformed my nymphs and incensed me. Thou have transformed them into shapes that lack the power to reason, and thou have incensed in me anger that is immortal and undying, for at one and the same time I am robbed of both my honor and my nymphs."

Cupid said:

"Ceres, thy nymphs were stubborn, and thyself, speaking so imperiously to Cupid, somewhat stately and arrogant.

"If you ask the cause in anger, I respond, *Sic volo, sic iubeo*: I wish this, and therefore I command this. In other words: I have the power here, not you.

"If you ask the cause in courtesy, I respond, *Quae venit ex merito poena dolenda venit*: When a punishment comes deservedly, it comes painfully.

"Thy nymphs were disdainful, and they have their just deserts.

"Thou, Ceres, govern just the guts of men, while I govern the hearts.

"With thy administered famine, thou seek to starve Erisichthon, whom his daughter shall preserve by my virtue: love."

"Thou are only a god, Cupid," Ceres said.

Cupid is a god, and Ceres is a goddess, and so they ought to be equal.

Cupid replied:

"No, Ceres, for I am such a god as makes thunder fall out of Jove's hand, by throwing thoughts into his heart, and to be more terrified by the sparkling of — the fire in — a lady's eye than men are terrified by the flashes of his — Jove's — lightning.

"I am such a god as has kindled more fire in Neptune's bosom than the whole sea that he is king of can quench.

"Such power have I that Pluto's never-dying fire only scorches in comparison to my flames."

Jove (Jupiter), Neptune, and Pluto are the three main Roman gods. Jupiter is the god of the sky, Neptune is the god of the sea, and Pluto is the god of the Land of the Dead, aka the Underworld. Jupiter is the king of the gods.

Cupid continued:

"Diana has felt some impulses of love, Vesta does feel some impulses of love, and Ceres shall feel some impulses of love."

Diana's Greek name is Artemis; she is the goddess of the hunt. Vesta's Greek name is Hestia; she is the goddess of the hearth. Both Diana and Vesta are virgin goddesses.

Diana, however, had once fallen in love with Orion, a hunter.

Ceres, of course, was the mother of Proserpine; their Greek names are Demeter and Persephone. Perhaps, however, Ceres had not yet become a mother at this time.

"Are thou so cruel?" Ceres asked.

Cupid replied, "To those who resist, I am a lion; to those who submit, I am a lamb."

"Can thou make such difference in passion, and yet shall it all be love?" Ceres asked.

When Cupid is a lion, love can be painful; when Cupid is a lamb, love can be pleasurable.

Cupid replied:

"Yes, as much difference as between sickness and health, although life is in both.

"Those who yield and honor Cupid shall possess sweet thoughts and enjoy pleasing wishes; the others shall be tormented with vain imaginations and impossible hopes."

"How may my nymphs be restored?" Ceres asked.

"If thou restore Erisichthon, if they embrace their loves, and if all offer sacrifice to me," Cupid said.

The nymph's loves are the foresters. So says Cupid.

Ceres objected, "Erisichthon did in contempt hew down my sacred tree."

"Thy nymphs did in disdain scorn my constant love," Cupid said.

"Erisichthon slew most cruelly my chaste Fidelia, whose blood lies yet on the ground," Ceres said.

"But Diana has changed her blood to fresh flowers, which are to be seen on the ground," Cupid said.

"What honor shall Erisichthon do to Ceres? What amends can he make to Fidelia?" Ceres asked.

"Erisichthon shall deck all of Ceres' grove with garlands, and he shall consider every tree holy," Cupid said. "He shall erect a stately monument in remembrance of Fidelia, and he shall offer to you a yearly sacrifice."

"What sacrifice shall I and my nymphs offer thee? For I will do anything to restore my nymphs and honor thee," Ceres asked.

Cupid said:

"You shall present in honor of my mother, Venus, grapes and wheat; for *Sine Cerere et Baccho friget Venus*."

"Grapes and wheat" mean "wine and food."

The Latin means "Without Ceres (goddess of agriculture) and Bacchus (god of wine), Venus (goddess of sexual passion) grows cold."

Cupid continued:

"You shall allow your nymphs to play, sometimes to be idle, in the favor of Cupid; for *Otia si tollas, periere Cupidinis arcus*."

The Latin means, "If you take away leisure, Cupid's bow is broken." This is line 139 of Ovid's *Remedia Amoris (Cures for Love)*.

Much falling in love takes place during leisure hours.

Cupid continued:

"That is for Ceres.

"Thy nymphs shall make no vows to continue to be virgins, nor use words to disgrace love, nor flee from opportunities that kindle affections.

"If they are chaste, let them not be cruel.

"If they are beautiful, let them not be proud.

"If they are loving, let them not be inconstant and disloyal.

"Cruelty is for tigers, pride is for peacocks, and inconstancy is for fools."

Ceres said, "Cupid, I yield, and the nymphs shall, but sweet Cupid, let them not be deceived by flattery, which takes on the shape of love; nor let them be deceived by lust, which is clothed in the habit — the garment — of love to delude, for men have as many tricks to use to delude as they have words to speak.

"Both flattery and lust disguise themselves as love, inwardly and outwardly."

"Those who practice deceit shall perish," Cupid said. "Cupid favors none but the faithful."

"Well, I will go to Erisichthon, and bring him before thee," Ceres said.

"Then thy nymphs shall recover their forms — their former shapes — as long as they yield to love," Cupid said.

"They shall," Ceres promised.

They exited.

— **5.2** —

Petulius and Protea stood in front of the temple of Cupid. Protea had told Petulius her story, including how she had gained the ability to shape-shift by sleeping with Neptune.

Petulius said, "Yours is a strange story, Protea, by which I find the gods become amorous, virgins become immortal, goddesses become full of cruelty, and men become full of unhappiness."

Neptune is the amorous god, Protea is the virgin who acquired an ability that usually only immortal gods and goddesses could have, Ceres is the goddess who became cruel, and Erisichthon is a man who became unhappy.

Protea said, "I have told both my father's misfortunes, grown by pride and arrogance, and my own misfortunes, grown by weakness. His pride and arrogance are shown by his thwarting of Ceres, and my weakness is shown by my yielding to Neptune."

Petulius said, "I know, Protea, that hard iron, falling into fire, grows soft; and then the tender heart of a virgin, being in love, must necessarily melt: for what should a fair, young, and witty lady answer to the sweet enticements of love, but *Molle meum levibus cor est violabile telit?*"

The Latin means, "My heart is tender, and it is easily pierced by [Cupid's] light shafts."

This is a quotation from Ovid's *Heroides* (*Heroines*) xv.79.

Petulius believed that Protea had been in love with Neptune.

Protea said, "I have heard, too, that the hearts of men, stiffer than steel, have by love been made softer than wool, and then they cry, *Omnia vincit amor, et nos cedamus amori.*"

The Latin means, "Love conquers all, and we will yield ourselves to love."

Protea believed that Petulius had been in love with the Siren.

The quotation is from Virgil's *Eclogues* (*Bucolics*), x, 69.

Bucolics are pastoral poems.

"Men have often feigned sighs," Petulius said.

"And women forged tears," Protea said.

"Suppose I don't love," Petulius said.

"Suppose I don't care," Protea said.

"If men swear and lie, how will you test their loves?" Petulius asked.

"If women swear they love, how will you test their dissembling?" Protea asked.

"The gods put wit into women," Petulius said.

That wit — intelligence — could be used to dissemble and lie more effectively.

"And nature put deceit into men," Protea said.

"I did this just to test your patience," Petulius said.

In other words: I said, 'Suppose I don't love,' just to test your patience.

"Nor did I mean it, except to test your faith," Protea said.

In other words: I said, 'Suppose I don't care,' just to test your faith.

A subtext of their badinage was Protea's sleeping with Neptune and Petulius' falling in love with the Siren.

Both forgave the other, and with good reason.

The gods can be very insistent when they want to sleep with mortal women, and they are very powerful. The gods have committed rape. At least Protea had gotten something from Neptune that was useful.

The Siren had the gift of enchantment in her song, and her song had enchanted Petulius.

Neither Protea nor Petulius had had a choice in what they had done.

Protea continued:

"But look, Petulius, what miraculous punishments here are for deserts in love:

"This rock was a nymph to Ceres; so was this rose; so was that bird."

"All are changed from their real shapes?" Petulius asked.

"All are changed by Cupid, because they disdained love, or because they dissembled in it," Protea said.

"This is a fair and clear warning to Protea," Petulius said. "I hope she will love without dissembling."

Protea said:

"This is an admonition for Petulius, so that he will not delude those who love him; for Cupid can also change men.

"Let us go into the temple."

The foresters — Ramis, Silvestris, and Montanus — stood in front of the temple of Cupid.

Ramis said, "This turns out luckily: Cupid has promised to restore our mistresses; and Ceres has promised that they shall accept our loves."

Montanus said, "I always imagined that true love would end
with sweet joys, even though it was begun with deep sighs."

Silvestris said, "But how shall we behave toward the nymphs when we shall see them smile when they regain their own shapes? We must meet with and face them, and perhaps they will frown."

"Tush!" Ramis said. "Let us endure the bending of their fair brows in frowns, and let us endure the scorching of their sparkling eyes, as long as we may possess at last the depth of their affections."

"Possess?" Montanus said. "Never doubt that we will because Ceres has restored Erisichthon to his former state, and therefore she will persuade the nymphs to love us — indeed, she will command them to love us."

"If the nymphs' love for us would come by commandment of Ceres, and not by the nymphs' own impulses, I would rather that they should hate us," Silvestris said, "for what joy can there be in our lives, or sweetness in our loves, when every kiss shall be sealed with a curse, and every kind word shall proceed out of fear, not affection? Enforcement is worse than enchantment."

Both should be rejected. Forced marriages are wrong, and getting someone to love you through the use of love spells or love potions — assuming they worked — would be wrong.

"Are thou so scrupulous and exacting in love, thou who were accustomed to be most unconcerned about love?" Ramis said. "Let them curse all day, as long as I may have just one kiss at night."

"Thou are worse than Silvestris," Montanus said. "He is not content without absolute love, and thou are content with indifferent and apathetic love."

Silvestris said, "But here comes Ceres with Erisichthon. Let us look grave; for in her heart, she hates us deeply."

Ceres wanted her nymphs to be changed back to their own forms, so Ceres had reason to be displeased with the foresters, who had requested that Cupid change the nymphs' forms into a stone, a flower, and a bird.

61

Ceres, Erisichthon, and Tirtena walked over to the foresters, who were in front of the temple of Cupid.

Erisichthon had been restored to his former state: He was no longer gaunt and famished.

"I will hallow and honor thy woods with solemn feasts, and I will honor all thy nymphs with due regard and respect," Erisichthon said to Ceres.

Ceres said:

"Well, do so, and thank Cupid who commands; and thank my foolish nymphs, who don't know how to obey."

The nymphs had disrespected Cupid, and so he had metamorphosed them. To free the nymphs, Ceres had been forced to restore Erisichthon to his former state.

Ceres continued:

"Here are the lovers ready at receipt."

"At receipt" was a hunting term. Hunters would be positioned in a place toward which game was driven. Here, the three foresters were the hunters, and the three nymphs were the game.

Ceres continued:

"How are you now, gentlemen? What do you seek?"

"Nothing but what Ceres would like to find," Ramis said.

Both Ceres and the foresters wanted the nymphs to be given back their former shapes.

"Ceres has found those whom I wish she had lost — foolish lovers," Ceres said.

The foolish lovers were the foresters.

"Ceres may lose those whom Cupid would save — true lovers," Ramis said.

"You think so one of another," Ceres said. "You think that each of you is a faithful lover."

"Cupid knows so of us all," Silvestris said.

"You might have made me a counselor of your loves," Ceres said.

She wanted to have known early about their loves. She could have advised them.

But lovers tend not to listen to advice. Think of a father telling a daughter, "These two boys are almost identical. If you must fall in love, fall in love with the one who has a job."

"Aye, madam, if love would admit counsel," Montanus said.

Since Ceres wanted virgins to serve her, she would have advised the foresters to fall in love with someone else. The foresters would not have taken that advice.

The temple doors opened, and Cupid came out of his temple.

Ceres said, "Cupid, here is Erisichthon in his former state; restore my nymphs to theirs, and then they shall embrace these lovers, who wither out their youth."

Petulius and Protea came out of the temple.

"Honored be mighty Cupid, who makes me live!" Erisichthon said.

"Honored be mighty Cupid, who makes me love—" Petulius said.

"— and me!" Protea said.

"What, yet more lovers?" Ceres said. "I think it is impossible for Ceres to have anyone follow her in one hour and not be in love in the next hour."

Cupid said:

"Erisichthon, be thou careful to honor Ceres, and don't forget to please her nymphs. The faithful love of thy daughter, Protea, has wrought both pity in me to grant her desires, and to release thy punishments.

"Thou, Petulius, shall enjoy thy love because I know thee to be loyal."

Petulius had fallen in love with the Siren, but as soon as he had heard the name "Protea," he had rejected the Siren's advances. That was quite an accomplishment, given the Siren's supernatural ability to attract men.

"Then shall Petulius be most happy," Petulius said.

"And Protea most fortunate," Protea said.

Cupid then asked:

"But do you, Ramis, continue your constant love?

"And you, Montanus?

"And you, Silvestris?"

Speaking for all the foresters, Ramis said, "Nothing can alter our loves, which increase while the means of fulfillment decrease, and grow stronger in being weakened."

Cupid said:

"Then, Venus, send down that shower, wherewith thou were accustomed to wash those who do the worship; and let love by thy beams be honored in all the world, and feared, wished for, and wondered at."

A shower fell, and the nymphs were metamorphosed back into their normal and natural shapes.

From a stone, Nisa became herself.

From a rose, Celia became herself.

From a bird, Niobe became herself.

Cupid then said:

"Here are thy nymphs, Ceres."

"Whom do I see? Nisa?" Ramis said.

"Divine Celia, more beautiful than she ever was!" Montanus said.

"My sweet Niobe!" Silvestris said.

Ceres said, "Why do you stare, my nymphs, as if you were amazed and bewildered? Triumph rather because you have your own shapes. This great god Cupid, who metamorphosed you because of your prides and follies, has by my prayer and promise restored you."

Cupid said:

"You see, ladies, what it is to make a mockery of love, or a scorn of Cupid."

One ought not to commit a misdeed that a god or goddess must and will punish.

Cupid continued:

"See where your lovers stand.

"You must now take them for your husbands: This is my judgment, and this is Ceres' promise."

Ramis said, "Happy Ramis!"

Montanus said, "Happy Montanus!"

Silvestris said, "Happy Silvestris!"

"Why don't you speak, nymphs?" Ceres said. "This must be done, and you must yield."

"Not I!" Nisa said.

"Nor I!" Niobe said.

"Nor I!" Celia said.

Ceres said, "You nymphs will not yield? Then Cupid in his fury shall turn you again into insentient, unfeeling, and shameful shapes."

Cupid asked:

"Won't you nymphs yield?

"What do you say, Ramis?

"Do your loves continue? Are your thoughts constant?

"And yours, Montanus?

"And yours, Silvestris?"

"My love is most unspotted and is pure!" Ramis said.

"And my love is the same!" Montanus said.

"And my love is the same, Cupid!" Silvestris said. "Nothing can alter that!"

"And won't you yield, virgins?" Cupid asked.

Nisa, who had been changed to a stone, said:

"Not I, Cupid!

"Neither do I thank thee that I have been restored to life, nor do I fear to again be changed to stone because I would rather be worn with the continual beating of waves than dulled and stupefied by the importunities and solicitations of men, whose open flatteries make way to their secret lusts, retaining as little truth in their hearts as modesty in their words.

"How happy was Nisa, who felt nothing. She was worn away, yet she did not feel the wasting away!

"Unfortunate wench, who now has ears to hear men's cunning lies, and eyes to behold men's dissembling looks!

"Change me, Cupid, again, into a stone, for I will not love!"

Ramis said, "Miserable Ramis! Unlucky in love; to change the lady, I was accursed; and now to lose her, I am desperate and without hope!"

Celia, who had been changed to a rose, said:

"Nor will I love, Cupid.

"Well would I content myself to bud in the summer, and to die in the winter because more good comes from the rose than can come from love.

"When the rose is fresh, it has a sweet scent of perfume; love, when it is young, has a sour taste.

"The rose, when it is old, does not lose its beneficial properties; love, when it is stale, grows loathsome.

"The rose, distilled with fire, yields sweet water: rose oil. Love, in extremities, kindles jealousies.

"In the rose, however it be and in whatever form it is, there is sweetness; in love, there is nothing but bitterness.

"If men look pale, and swear, and sigh, then truly women 'must' yield, because men say they love, as though our hearts were tied to their tongues, and we must choose them by their command, ourselves feeling no affection and love, and so have our thoughts bound like apprentices to their words.

"Change me again into a rose.

"I will not yield!"

Montanus said, referring to himself in the second person:

"Which way shall thou turn and direct thyself, since nothing will turn and change her heart and affections?

"Die, Montanus, with shame and grief, and both infinite!"

Niobe, who had been changed to a bird, said:

"Nor will I love, Cupid!

"Let me hang always in the air, which I found more constant than men's words.

"Happy Niobe, who did not touch the ground where they walk, but always holding thy beak in the air, did never turn back to behold the earth.

"In the heavens I saw an orderly course, in the earth I saw nothing but disorderly, unruly love and peevishness and foolishness.

"Change me again into a bird, Cupid, for I will not yield!"

Silvestris said, "I wish that I myself were stone, flower, or bird, seeing that Niobe has a heart harder than stone, a face fairer than the rose, and a mind lighter than feathers."

"Lighter" can mean 1) less heavy, and 2) more wanton.

Cupid said:

"What have we here? Has punishment made you nymphs perverse?

"Ceres, I vow here by my sweet mother Venus, that if they do not yield, I will turn them again, not into flowers, or stones, or birds, but into monsters, no less filthy to be seen than to be called hateful: They shall creep who now stand, and they shall be to all men odious, and they shall be to themselves (for their mind they shall retain) loathsome."

This was not an idle threat: The gods sometimes did change young women into monsters.

The minor sea-god Gaucus loved a beautiful young woman named Scylla, but the goddess sorceress Circe also loved Glaucus. Driven by jealousy, Circe transformed Scylla into a monster. Scylla had six long necks. Each neck was like a serpent with a serpent's head at the end. She used her necks to seize and devour one of Odysseus' men with each neck.

Ceres said, "My sweet nymphs, for the honor of your sex, for the love of Ceres, out of respect for your own country, yield to love. Yield, my sweet nymphs, to sweet love."

Nisa said, "Shall I yield to him who plotted my destruction, and when his love was hottest, caused me to be changed to a rock?"

Ramis said, "Nisa, the extremity of love is madness, and to be mad is to be senseless; upon that rock I resolved to end my life. Fair Nisa, forgive him — me — thy change, who for himself provided a worse fate."

Celia said, "Shall I yield to him who made so small account of my beauty that he studied and contrived how he might never behold it again?"

Montanus said, "Fair lady, in the rose I always did behold thy color, and I resolved by continual gazing to perish, which I could not do when thou were in thine own shape because thou were so coy and aloof and swift in flying from me."

Niobe said, "Shall I yield to him who caused me to have wings, so that I might fly farther from him?"

Silvestris said, "Sweet Niobe, the farther you did seem to be from me, the nearer I was to my death, which, to make it speedier, I wished for thee to have wings to fly into the air, and for myself I wished lead on my heels so I could sink into the sea."

"Well, my good nymphs, yield," Ceres said. "Let Ceres entreat you to yield."

Nisa said, "I am content to yield, as long as Ramis, when he finds me cold in love, or recalcitrant, attributes it to his own folly, in that I retain some nature of the rock he changed me into."

Ramis said, "O, my sweet Nisa! Be what thou will, and let all thy imperfections be excused by me, as long as thou just say thou love me."

"I do," Nisa said.

Ramis said, "Happy Ramis!"

Celia said, "I consent to yield, as long as Montanus, when in the midst of his sweet delight, shall find some bitter rebuffs from me, shall impute it to his folly, in that he allowed me to be a rose that has thorns to go with her pleasantness, as he is likely to have along with my love some shrewishness."

Montanus said, "Let me bleed every minute with the thorns of the rose, as long as I may enjoy the perfume of the rose for just one hour. Love me, fair Celia, and at thy pleasure comfort me, and confound me."

"I do," Celia said.

Montanus said, "Fortunate Montanus!"

Niobe said:

"I yielded first in my mind, although my usual practice is to be last to speak. But if Silvestris should find me not ever at home, let him curse himself who gave me wings to fly away from home; whose feathers, if his jealousy shall break them, my policy shall imp."

To "imp" is to mend a wing by grafting feathers.

Niobe continued:

"*Non custodiri, ni velit, ulla potest.*"

The Latin means, "No guard can be set over a woman's will."

The quotation is from Ovid's *Amores* (*Loves*) iii.4,6.

Silvestris said:

"My sweet Niobe! Fly to wherever thou will all day. As long as I may find thee in my nest at night, I will love thee and believe thee.

"*Sit modo, non feci, dicere lingua memor.*"

The Latin means, "Let your tongue only remember to say, I did not do it."

The quotation is from Ovid's *Amores* (*Loves*) iii.14,48.

Cupid said:

"I am glad you are all agreed; enjoy your loves, and everyone enjoy his delight.

"Thou, Erisichthon, are restored by Ceres, and all the lovers are pleased by Cupid. Ceres is joyful, and I am honored.

"Now, ladies, I will make such unspotted love among you that there shall be no suspicion or argument, no unkindness or jealousy, but let all ladies hereafter take heed that they do not resist love, which works wonders."

"I will charm and bewitch my nymphs, so that they shall neither be so haughty that they will not bow to love, nor so light and wanton as immediately to yield," Ceres said.

Cupid said:

"Here is no one who is not happy, but don't do as Hippomanes did, when by Venus' aid he won Atalanta: Don't defile her temple with unchaste desires, and don't forget to sacrifice and keep his vows."

Atalanta was a fleet-footed woman who did not wish to marry. Bothered by the many men seeking to marry her, she made each of them agree to run a footrace with her. If he won the footrace, he would marry her. If she won the footrace, he would be killed. Many men died.

Hippomanes wanted to marry her, and he got help from Venus, who gave him three golden apples. During the race, three times he threw a golden apple to the ground, and Atalanta took the time to chase after and pick up each gold apple, all of which weighed her down.

Hippomanes won the race and married Atalanta, but he made an enemy out of Venus by having newlywed sex with Atalanta in Venus' temple and by neglecting to sacrifice to Venus.

In another version of the myth, Hippomanes had newlywed sex with Atalanta in a cave near the temple of Cybele, and Cybele became angry at them.

Cupid continued:

"I will soar up into heaven, to settle the loves of the gods, I who on earth have disposed the affections of men."

Ceres said:

"I will go to my harvest, whose corn has now come out of the blade — the flat leaf — into the ear.

"Let all this amorous troop proceed to the temple of Venus, there to consummate what Cupid has commanded."

The consummation of the marriage is different from the wedding. Ceres meant for the couples to be married in the temple of Venus and to consummate the marriages elsewhere. Otherwise, they would make an enemy of Venus.

"To consummate" can mean 1) to complete, 2) to carry out, and 3) to accomplish.

Erisichthon said:

"I, in the honor of Cupid and Ceres, will solemnize this feast within my house; and learn, if it is not too late, again to love.

"But you foresters were unkind, because in all my maladies you would not visit me."

"Thou know, Erisichthon, that lovers visit none but their mistresses," Montanus said.

This isn't a good excuse; in fact, Montanus had been afraid to visit Erisichthon because he might be affected by Erisichthon's curse.

"Well, I will not take it unkindly, since all ends in kindness," Erisichthon said.

This showed a change in Erisichthon. Rather than being arrogant, he quickly accepted Montanus' poor excuse for the foresters not visiting him.

Ceres said:

"Let it be so.

"These lovers attend to nothing that we say."

"Yes, we do attend to what Ceres says," Ramis said.

"Well, do," Ceres said.

NOTES

— 1.1 —

For Your Information:

Erysichthon once ordered all trees in the sacred grove of Demeter to be cut down. One huge oak was covered with votive wreaths, a symbol of every prayer Demeter had granted, and so the men refused to cut it down. Erysichthon grabbed an axe and cut it down himself, killing a dryad nymph in the process. The nymph's dying words were a curse on Erysichthon.

Demeter responded to the nymph's curse and punished him by entreating Limos (here a female deity), the spirit of unrelenting and insatiable hunger, to place herself in his stomach. Food acted like fuel on a fire: The more he ate, the hungrier he got. Erysichthon sold all his possessions to buy food, but was still hungry. At last he sold his own daughter Mestra into slavery. The latter was freed from slavery by her former lover Poseidon, who gave her the gift of shape-shifting into any creature at will to escape her bonds. Erysichthon used her shape-shifting ability to sell her numerous times to make money to feed himself, but no amount of food was enough. Eventually, Erysichthon ate himself in hunger. Nothing of him remained the following morning.

Source: "Erisichthon of Thessaly." Wikipedia. Accessed 18 September 2022

https://en.wikipedia.org/wiki/Erysichthon_of_Thessaly

NOTE: Demeter's Roman name is Ceres. Poseidon's Roman name is Neptune.

— 1.1 —

For Your Information:

Aglaonice or Aganice of Thessaly was a Greek astronomer and thaumaturge of the 2nd or 1st century BC. She is mentioned in the writings of Plutarch and in the scholia to Apollonius of Rhodes as a female astronomer and as the daughter of Hegetor (or Hegemon) of Thessaly. She was regarded as a sorceress for (amongst other extraordinary feats) her (self-proclaimed) ability to 'make the moon disappear from the sky' which has been taken — first by Plutarch and subsequently by modern astronomers — to mean that she could predict the time and general area where a lunar eclipse would occur.

A Greek proverb makes reference to Aglaonice's alleged boasting: "Yes, as the Moon obeys Aglaonice". A number of female astrologers, apparently regarded as sorcerers, were associated with Aglaonice. They were known as the "witches of Thessaly" and were active from the 3rd to 1st centuries BCE.

Source of Above: "Aglaonice." Wikipedia. Accessed on 18 September 2022 https://en.wikipedia.org/wiki/Aglaonice

— 2.1 —

For Your Information:

> *In Jewish law, sex is not considered shameful, sinful or obscene. Sex is not thought of as a necessary evil for the sole purpose of procreation. Although sexual desire comes from the yetzer ra (the evil impulse), it is no more evil than hunger or thirst, which also come from the yetzer ra. Like hunger, thirst or other basic instincts, sexual desire must be controlled and channeled, satisfied at the proper time, place and manner. But when sexual desire is satisfied between a husband and wife at the proper time, out of mutual love and desire, sex is a mitzvah.*

Source: "Kosher Sex." Judaism 101.
https://www.jewfaq.org/kosher_sex

— 3.2 —

The Aaron Hill poem is from this source:
  William Stanley Braithwaite, ed. *The Book of Georgian Verse*. 1909.
  https://www.bartleby.com/333/93.html

"Agelastos" is Latin for "unsmiling," and it was the nickname of Marcus Licinius Crassus, who laughed just once in his life. The story is that rich Romans regarded thistles, properly prepared, as a delicacy, and they would not allow poor Romans to eat them. Agelastos laughed when he saw an ass eating thistles for free.

Eating thistles is a way of roughly handling them.

Nettles and thistles both irritate, but they are different plants. Nettles have tiny hairs that sting, and thistles have leaves with sharp prickles.

Thistles are a symbol of Scotland, and "he which touchest the [thistle] tenderly is soonest stung" could be advice to face Scottish raiders bravely and punish them.

For Your Information:

II. That Crassus never laughed but once, and that was at an Asse eating Thistles, seems strange to the Doctor, yet he gives no reason for this, but only that the object was unridiculous, & that laughter is not meerly voluntary. But these are no reasons: for a more ridiculous object there cannot be, then to see such a medley of pleasure and pain in the Asses eating of Thistles; for whilst he bites them, they prick him, so that his tongue must needs be pricked, though perhaps his lips may be hard, and not so easily penetrable; when arose the Proverb, Like lips, like lettice. But there was something else in this that moved Crassus to laugh: For he saw here the vanity both of most men taking pleasure in those things which are accompanied with much pain and sorrow: Besides, he saw here the folly of the Roman rich men, who held Thistles for such a dainty dish, that they would not suffer poor men to eat thereof, engrossing them with great summes of money to themselves, which notwithstanding the Asses did eat on free cost. Was it not then a ridiculous thing to see rich men pay so dear for Asses food, and to debarre poore men from that meat which they permitted to Asses?

Source of Above:

Alexander Ross (1652) *Arcana Microcosmi*, Book II, Chapter 15, pp. 174-179.

https://penelope.uchicago.edu/ross/ross215.html#9

https://medium.com/equestrian-explorers/what-did-the-ancient-romans-eat-9ba2b595046c

The below information comes from "The History of Artichokes":

Thistles—in the form of artichokes and cardoons—have been on the human table since at least the days of ancient Greece and Rome.

[...]

Both today's cultivated artichoke and cardoon are, scientists believe, descended from the wild cardoon, a tougher, meaner, and pricklier plant, likely a native of north Africa and Sicily. Pliny the Elder mentions two types of edible thistles known to first-century Romans: one which "throws out numerous stalks immediately it leaves the ground," which sounds like a cardoon; the other "thicker, and having but a single stem" and purple flowers, which may be a progenitor of the modern globe artichoke. This last, according to Pliny, had a number of beneficial medicinal effects, among them curing baldness, strengthening the stomach, freshening the breath, and promoting the conception of boys. Though Pliny doesn't mention it, it was also purportedly an aphrodisiac. The Roman ate them pickled in honey and vinegar, and seasoned with cumin.

[...]

Similarly, wild thistles—the atrociously spiny stuff Winnie-the-Pooh's doleful donkey Eeyore munches in his Gloomy Place—are said to have edible (even delicious) leaf ribs. I personally can't attest to this, but even devoted wild-food aficionados agree that wild thistle is a challenge to gather, unless you happen to be wandering through the woods wearing elbow-length leather gloves.

Source of Above: Rupp, Rebecca, "The History of Artichokes." *National Geographic.* 12 November 2014
https://www.nationalgeographic.com/culture/article/artichokes

— 4.2 —

For Your Information:

Sirens are not the same as mermaids. Mermaids are half-fish women, but sirens (the ones with the hypnotic singing voices) are half-bird women from Greek mythology. On the other hand, sirens and mermaids have been conflated for a long time. When did it begin?

Sirens first appear in Homer's Odyssey in the 8th century B.C. Homer doesn't really describe them at all. All we know is that their song will ensnare anyone who hears it. [...]

Meanwhile, fish-tailed people were a subject of art for a long time. They showed up in Mesopotamian art at least from the Old Babylonian Period (c. 1830 BC – c. 1531 BC). These were usually men, like the god Ea, but fish-tailed women sometimes appeared.

Then in medieval times, sirens stopped being bird-ladies and became fish-ladies. But birds and fish aren't typically interchangeable. What happened? [...]

By the 14th century, the siren's identity had become standardized as a fish-tailed temptress with a hypnotic voice. The words siren and mermaid were interchangeable. [...]

Source of Above: "Fish or Fowl: How did Sirens become Mermaids?" Writing in Margins. 11/12/2018

https://writinginmargins.weebly.com/home/fish-or-fowl-how-did-sirens-become-mermaids

— 4.2 —

This is from my retelling of the *Argonautica*:

> *Soon, they reached the island of the Sirens, whose mother had been the muse Terpsichore. The Sirens were part bird and part human female. They sang, and the beauty of their singing led sailors to forget their homecoming and instead stay with the Sirens and listen to their songs while forgetting to eat and slowly starving to death.*
>
> *Orpheus realized the danger that the Argonauts were in, and so he started to play his lyre and sing in competition with the Sirens. His song was loud and lively, and it mostly drowned out the song of the Sirens. The current and the wind swept the Argo past the Sirens. Only one Argonaut — Butes, who loved battle — jumped overboard to swim to the Sirens. The goddess Aphrodite felt pity for him and rescued him and set him on shore far from the Sirens.*

Source of Above: David Bruce. *Jason and the Argonauts: A Retelling in Prose of Apollonius of Rhodes'* Argonautica.

This is from my retelling of the *Odyssey*. The speaker is Odysseus:

> *"When Circe finished speaking to me, dawn arrived, and I went directly to my ship and we set sail. Circe sent us a favorable wind to help us on our way. I told my crewmembers, 'I will tell you everything — everything that Circe told me. Dangers await us. We will come to the island of the Sirens. Circe said that only I would hear their song. You must tie me to the mast so that I cannot jump overboard, swim to their island, and die.' I did not tell them everything, as I had promised. I did not tell them about Scylla — I feared a mutiny.*
>
> *"As we approached the island of the Sirens, I melted beeswax and stopped the ears of the crewmembers with it so that they could not hear the song of the Sirens. They tied me tightly to the mast. I heard the song of the Sirens: 'Come to us, Odysseus. Your fame has reached the sky.*

79

Hear our song and become wise. We know what happened at Troy, and we know what will happen on the Earth.'

"I wanted my crewmembers to untie me. They tied me tighter to the mast. They rowed quickly to escape from danger. Once we were past the island of the Sirens, they removed the beeswax from their ears and untied me."

Source: David Bruce. *Homer's Odyssey: A Retelling in Prose.*

— **5.4** —

For Your Information:

The Wikipedia article on "Scylla" states that a beautiful young woman named

> *[...] Scylla was loved by [the sea-god] Glaucus, but Glaucus himself was also loved by the goddess sorceress Circe. While Scylla was bathing in the sea, the jealous Circe poured a baleful potion into the sea water which caused Scylla to transform into a frightful monster with four eyes and six long snaky necks equipped with grisly heads, each of which contained three rows of sharp shark's teeth. Her body consisted of 12 tentacle-like legs and a cat's tail, while six dog's heads ringed her waist. In this form, she attacked the ships of passing sailors, seizing one of the crew with each of her heads.*

Source of Above:

"Scylla." Wikipedia. Accessed 27 September 2022

https://en.wikipedia.org/wiki/Scylla

Wikipedia's source for the information is

Gaius Julius Hyginus, *Fabulae*, 199

As you can see below, the Wikipedia paragraph contains information not found in Gaius Julius Hyginus, *Fabulae*, 199. Wikipedia may be conflating Scylla, daughter of the River Crataeis, with Scylla, the daughter of Nisus, and Scylla, the daughter of Typhon. All of these Scyllas are mentioned in the *Fabulae*. It should be noted that myths are frequently inconsistent.

> § 199 THE OTHER SCYLLA: Scylla, daughter of the River Crataeis, is said to have been a most beautiful maiden. Glaucus loved her, but Circe, daughter of Sol, loved Glaucus. Since Scylla was accustomed to bathe in the sea, Circe, daughter of Sol, out of jealousy poisoned the water with drugs, and when Scylla went down into it, dogs sprang from her thighs, and she was made a monster. She avenged her injuries, for as Ulysses sailed by, she robbed him of his companions.

Source of Above: Gaius Julius Hyginus, *Fabulae*, 199. Translated by Mary Grant. TOPOS text. Public Domain.

Hyginus, *Fabulae* from *The Myths of Hyginus*, translated and edited by Mary Grant. University of Kansas Publications in Humanistic Studies, no. 34., now in the public domain, with thanks to www.theoi.com for making the text available on line.

https://topostext.org/work/206

In Homer's *Odyssey*, Scylla has six long necks. Later myth stated that Scylla had once been a beautiful woman.

Below is an excerpt from my retelling of Homer's *Odyssey*. The speaker is Odysseus:

"We avoided the Crashing Rocks — we went the other route, the one that lay between Scylla and Charybdis. I told my men, 'We will get through this alive. You see the whirlpool. Stay clear of it. Sail close to this cliff, away from the whirlpool.' I did not mention Scylla. I remembered that Circe had told me that it was useless to try to stop Scylla from devouring six of my men, but I put on my armor, got my spears, and watched and waited. We saw Charybdis suck water down, down, down, and then vomit it up again. While we were watching Charybdis, Scylla struck. Each of her six long necks snaked down from her lair and grabbed one of my men. They shrieked my name, they screamed for help, but I could do nothing. She ate them raw. I have seen much evil in my life, but this made me feel the worst.

Source: David Bruce. *Homer's Odyssey: A Retelling in Prose.*

APPENDIX A: FAIR USE

§ 107. Limitations on exclusive rights: Fair use
　　Release date: 2004-04-30

Notwithstanding the provisions of sections 106 and 106A, the fair use of a copyrighted work, including such use by reproduction in copies or phonorecords or by any other means specified by that section, for purposes such as criticism, comment, news reporting, teaching (including multiple copies for classroom use), scholarship, or research, is not an infringement of copyright. In determining whether the use made of a work in any particular case is a fair use the factors to be considered shall include —

(1) the purpose and character of the use, including whether such use is of a commercial nature or is for nonprofit educational purposes;

(2) the nature of the copyrighted work;

(3) the amount and substantiality of the portion used in relation to the copyrighted work as a whole; and

(4) the effect of the use upon the potential market for or value of the copyrighted work.

The fact that a work is unpublished shall not itself bar a finding of fair use if such finding is made upon consideration of all the above factors.

Source of Fair Use information:

<http://www.law.cornell.edu/uscode/17/107.html>

APPENDIX B: ABOUT THE AUTHOR

It was a dark and stormy night. Suddenly a cry rang out, and on a hot summer night in 1954, Josephine, wife of Carl Bruce, gave birth to a boy — me. Unfortunately, this young married couple allowed Reuben Saturday, Josephine's brother, to name their first-born. Reuben, aka "The Joker," decided that Bruce was a nice name, so he decided to name me Bruce Bruce. I have gone by my middle name — David — ever since.

Being named Bruce David Bruce hasn't been all bad. Bank tellers remember me very quickly, so I don't often have to show an ID. It can be fun in charades, also. When I was a counselor as a teenager at Camp Echoing Hills in Warsaw, Ohio, a fellow counselor gave the signs for "sounds like" and "two words," then she pointed to a bruise on her leg twice. Bruise Bruise? Oh yeah, Bruce Bruce is the answer!

Uncle Reuben, by the way, gave me a haircut when I was in kindergarten. He cut my hair short and shaved a small bald spot on the back of my head. My mother wouldn't let me go to school until the bald spot grew out again.

Of all my brothers and sisters (six in all), I am the only transplant to Athens, Ohio. I was born in Newark, Ohio, and have lived all around Southeastern Ohio. However, I moved to Athens to go to Ohio University and have never left.

At Ohio U, I never could make up my mind whether to major in English or Philosophy, so I got a bachelor's degree with a double major in both areas, then I added a Master of Arts degree in English and a Master of Arts degree in Philosophy. Yes, I have my MAMA degree.

Currently, and for a long time to come (I eat fruits and veggies), I am spending my retirement writing books such as *Nadia Comaneci: Perfect 10*, *The Funniest People in Comedy*, *Homer's* Iliad: *A Retelling in Prose*, and *William Shakespeare's* Hamlet: *A Retelling in Prose*.

If all goes well, I will publish one or two books a year for the rest of my life. (On the other hand, a good way to make God laugh is to tell Her your plans.)

By the way, my sister Brenda Kennedy writes romances such as *A New Beginning* and *Shattered Dreams*.

APPENDIX C: SOME BOOKS BY DAVID BRUCE

Retellings of a Classic Work of Literature

Arden of Faversham: *A Retelling*

Ben Jonson's The Alchemist: *A Retelling*

Ben Jonson's The Arraignment, or Poetaster: *A Retelling*

Ben Jonson's Bartholomew Fair: *A Retelling*

Ben Jonson's The Case is Altered: *A Retelling*

Ben Jonson's Catiline's Conspiracy: *A Retelling*

Ben Jonson's The Devil is an Ass: *A Retelling*

Ben Jonson's Epicene: *A Retelling*

Ben Jonson's Every Man in His Humor: *A Retelling*

Ben Jonson's Every Man Out of His Humor: *A Retelling*

Ben Jonson's The Fountain of Self-Love, or Cynthia's Revels: *A Retelling*

Ben Jonson's The Magnetic Lady, or Humors Reconciled: *A Retelling*

Ben Jonson's The New Inn, or The Light Heart: *A Retelling*

Ben Jonson's Sejanus' Fall: *A Retelling*

Ben Jonson's The Staple of News: *A Retelling*

Ben Jonson's A Tale of a Tub: *A Retelling*

Ben Jonson's Volpone, or the Fox: *A Retelling*

Christopher Marlowe's Complete Plays: Retellings

Christopher Marlowe's Dido, Queen of Carthage: *A Retelling*

Christopher Marlowe's Doctor Faustus: *Retellings of the 1604 A-Text and of the 1616 B-Text*

Christopher Marlowe's Edward II: *A Retelling*

Christopher Marlowe's The Massacre at Paris: *A Retelling*

Christopher Marlowe's The Rich Jew of Malta: *A Retelling*

Christopher Marlowe's Tamburlaine, Parts 1 and 2: *Retellings*

Dante's Divine Comedy: *A Retelling in Prose*

Dante's Inferno: *A Retelling in Prose*

Dante's Purgatory: *A Retelling in Prose*

Dante's Paradise: *A Retelling in Prose*

The Famous Victories of Henry V: *A Retelling*

From the Iliad *to the* Odyssey: *A Retelling in Prose of Quintus of Smyrna's* Posthomerica

George Chapman, Ben Jonson, and John Marston's Eastward Ho! *A Retelling*

George Peele's The Arraignment of Paris: *A Retelling*

George Peele's The Battle of Alcazar: *A Retelling*

George Peele's David and Bathsheba, and the Tragedy of Absalom: *A Retelling*

George Peele's Edward I: *A Retelling*

George Peele's The Old Wives' Tale: *A Retelling*

George-a-Greene: *A Retelling*

The History of King Leir: *A Retelling*

Homer's Iliad: *A Retelling in Prose*

Homer's Odyssey: *A Retelling in Prose*

J.W. Gent.'s The Valiant Scot: *A Retelling*

Jason and the Argonauts: A Retelling in Prose of Apollonius of Rhodes' Argonautica

John Ford: Eight Plays Translated into Modern English

John Ford's The Broken Heart: *A Retelling*

John Ford's The Fancies, Chaste and Noble: *A Retelling*

John Ford's The Lady's Trial: *A Retelling*

John Ford's The Lover's Melancholy: *A Retelling*

John Ford's Love's Sacrifice: *A Retelling*

John Ford's Perkin Warbeck: *A Retelling*

John Ford's The Queen: *A Retelling*

John Ford's 'Tis Pity She's a Whore: *A Retelling*

John Lyly's Campaspe: *A Retelling*

John Lyly's Endymion, The Man in the Moon: *A Retelling*

John Lyly's Galatea: *A Retelling*

John Lyly's Love's Metamorphosis: *A Retelling*

John Lyly's Midas: *A Retelling*

John Lyly's Mother Bombie: *A Retelling*

John Lyly's Sappho and Phao: *A Retelling*

John Lyly's The Woman in the Moon: *A Retelling*

John Webster's The White Devil: *A Retelling*

King Edward III: *A Retelling*

Mankind: *A Medieval Morality Play* (A Retelling)

Margaret Cavendish's The Unnatural Tragedy: *A Retelling*

The Merry Devil of Edmonton: *A Retelling*

The Summoning of Everyman: *A Medieval Morality Play* (A Retelling)

Robert Greene's Friar Bacon and Friar Bungay: *A Retelling*

The Taming of a Shrew: *A Retelling*

Tarlton's Jests: A Retelling

Thomas Middleton's A Chaste Maid in Cheapside: *A Retelling*

Thomas Middleton's Women Beware Women: *A Retelling*

Thomas Middleton and Thomas Dekker's The Roaring Girl: *A Retelling*

Thomas Middleton and William Rowley's The Changeling: *A Retelling*

The Trojan War and Its Aftermath: Four Ancient Epic Poems

Virgil's Aeneid: *A Retelling in Prose*

William Shakespeare's 5 Late Romances: Retellings in Prose

William Shakespeare's 10 Histories: Retellings in Prose

William Shakespeare's 11 Tragedies: Retellings in Prose

William Shakespeare's 12 Comedies: Retellings in Prose

William Shakespeare's 38 Plays: Retellings in Prose
William Shakespeare's 1 Henry IV, aka Henry IV, Part 1: *A Retelling in Prose*
William Shakespeare's 2 Henry IV, aka Henry IV, Part 2: *A Retelling in Prose*
William Shakespeare's 1 Henry VI, aka Henry VI, Part 1: *A Retelling in Prose*
William Shakespeare's 2 Henry VI, aka Henry VI, Part 2: *A Retelling in Prose*
William Shakespeare's 3 Henry VI, aka Henry VI, Part 3: *A Retelling in Prose*
William Shakespeare's All's Well that Ends Well: *A Retelling in Prose*
William Shakespeare's Antony and Cleopatra: *A Retelling in Prose*
William Shakespeare's As You Like It: *A Retelling in Prose*
William Shakespeare's The Comedy of Errors: *A Retelling in Prose*
William Shakespeare's Coriolanus: *A Retelling in Prose*
William Shakespeare's Cymbeline: *A Retelling in Prose*
William Shakespeare's Hamlet: *A Retelling in Prose*
William Shakespeare's Henry V: *A Retelling in Prose*
William Shakespeare's Henry VIII: *A Retelling in Prose*
William Shakespeare's Julius Caesar: *A Retelling in Prose*
William Shakespeare's King John: *A Retelling in Prose*
William Shakespeare's King Lear: *A Retelling in Prose*
William Shakespeare's Love's Labor's Lost: *A Retelling in Prose*
William Shakespeare's Macbeth: *A Retelling in Prose*
William Shakespeare's Measure for Measure: *A Retelling in Prose*
William Shakespeare's The Merchant of Venice: *A Retelling in Prose*
William Shakespeare's The Merry Wives of Windsor: *A Retelling in Prose*
William Shakespeare's A Midsummer Night's Dream: *A Retelling in Prose*
William Shakespeare's Much Ado About Nothing: *A Retelling in Prose*
William Shakespeare's Othello: *A Retelling in Prose*
William Shakespeare's Pericles, Prince of Tyre: *A Retelling in Prose*
William Shakespeare's Richard II: *A Retelling in Prose*
William Shakespeare's Richard III: *A Retelling in Prose*
William Shakespeare's Romeo and Juliet: *A Retelling in Prose*
William Shakespeare's The Taming of the Shrew: *A Retelling in Prose*
William Shakespeare's The Tempest: *A Retelling in Prose*
William Shakespeare's Timon of Athens: *A Retelling in Prose*
William Shakespeare's Titus Andronicus: *A Retelling in Prose*
William Shakespeare's Troilus and Cressida: *A Retelling in Prose*
William Shakespeare's Twelfth Night: *A Retelling in Prose*
William Shakespeare's The Two Gentlemen of Verona: *A Retelling in Prose*
William Shakespeare's The Two Noble Kinsmen: *A Retelling in Prose*
William Shakespeare's The Winter's Tale: *A Retelling in Prose*